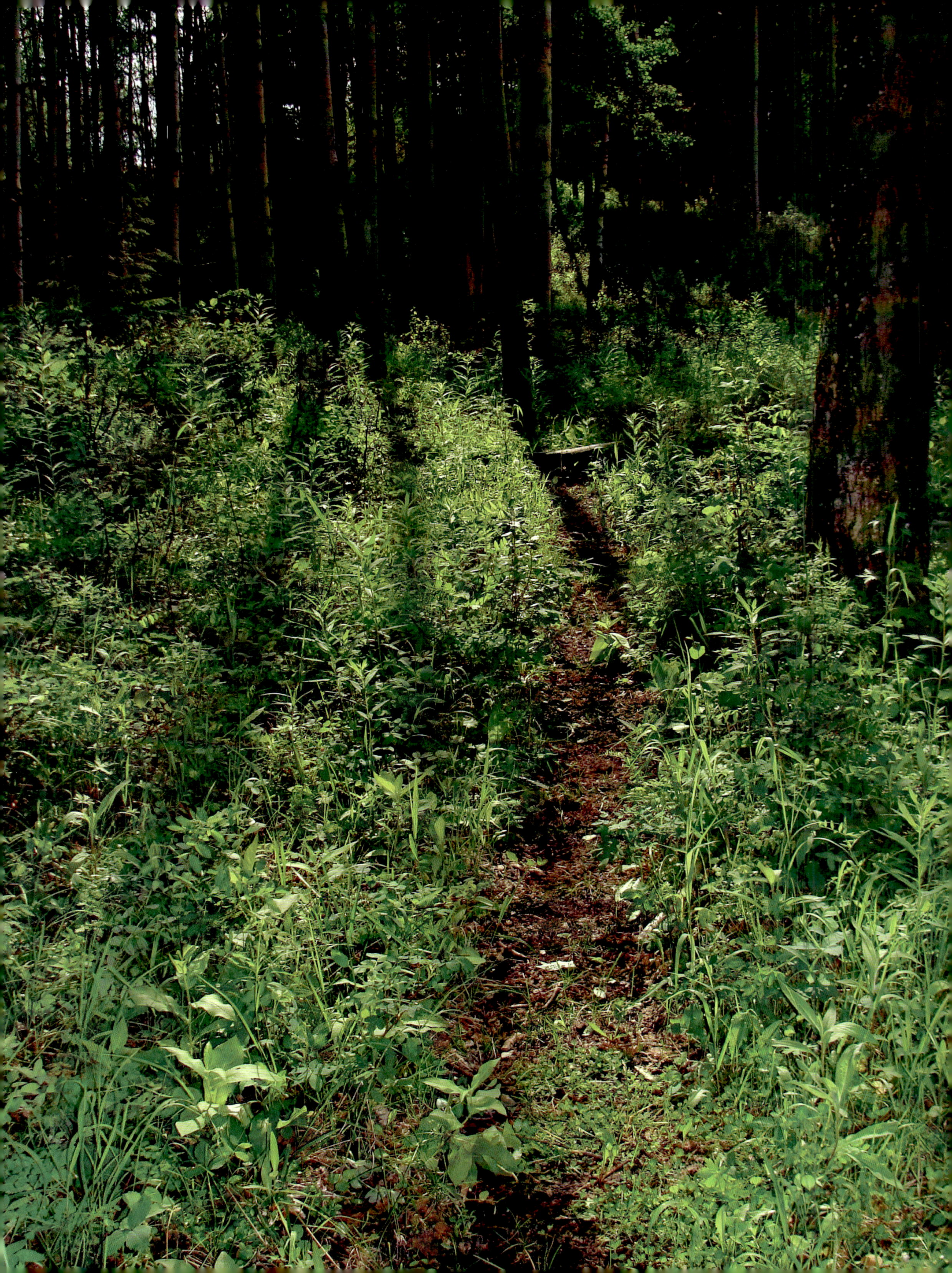

Look A Little Closer

A Photographer Sees God's Handwork in the Forest

Words & Photographs by Myrna Joanne Lieuwen

Author
Myrna Lieuwen

HighWay
A Division of Anomalos Publishing House
Crane

HighWay
A division of Anomalos Publishing House
Crane, 65633

Printed in the United States of America
10 1
ISBN-10: 0984260552 (hardback)
ISBN-13: 978-0984260553 (hardback)

All photography by the author, Myrna Joanne Lieuwen
Cover and book design by Daniel M. Wright

A CIP catalog record for this book is available from the Library of Congress.

Author contact email: *toploons@telus.net*

DEDICATION

To our Creator God, who has given us the gift
of the natural world to enjoy and take care of.

All thanks and praise to Him!

This work is also dedicated with love to my family:
Bob, Orrin, Jackie, Randy, and April

ACKNOWLEDGEMENTS

Thanks Candy, for your encouragement and
helping me to believe this book was a good idea.

Thanks, Marnie and Jen (my sisters) for the fun and excitement
while brainstorming with me and helping me to get started.

I am very grateful to Donna and Daniel from
Anomalos Publishing for their work on the book,
and their guidance to a beginner and especially
Donna for her patience with my inexperience.

INTRODUCTION

Many people testify that being in nature is often therapeutic. I have found this to be true for myself. Even as a young teenager, I would head for the woods when dealing with hurt or frustration. I often returned from my walk with a sense of having sorted through the emotions. My young heart seemed to know that God was always waiting to help me with my little problems, as I would pray and seek Him in the woods.

When I bought my first camera (also as a youth), I soon discovered the joy of photography. It became apparent that the bulk of my photos were of nature. Now I am a grown-up, a wife, and a mother. Though I am happy and content in that role, the cares of life still drive me to the forest. When I am stressed, weary, or upset at others or myself, I need to walk, and a new photo capturing a little piece of nature often brings delight and amazement. I know God is everywhere and will care wherever we are, but I have often been especially blessed by His presence when amongst the beauty and incredible diversity of the natural world. One of my favorite hobbies is still nature photography; sometimes the closer the better.

The woods are so full of treasures to be observed and enjoyed, and I am in awe of God's artistry whenever I take the time to observe things more closely. My hope is that this book will help people notice a few of the gifts, and grow closer to the Wonderful Giver of them.

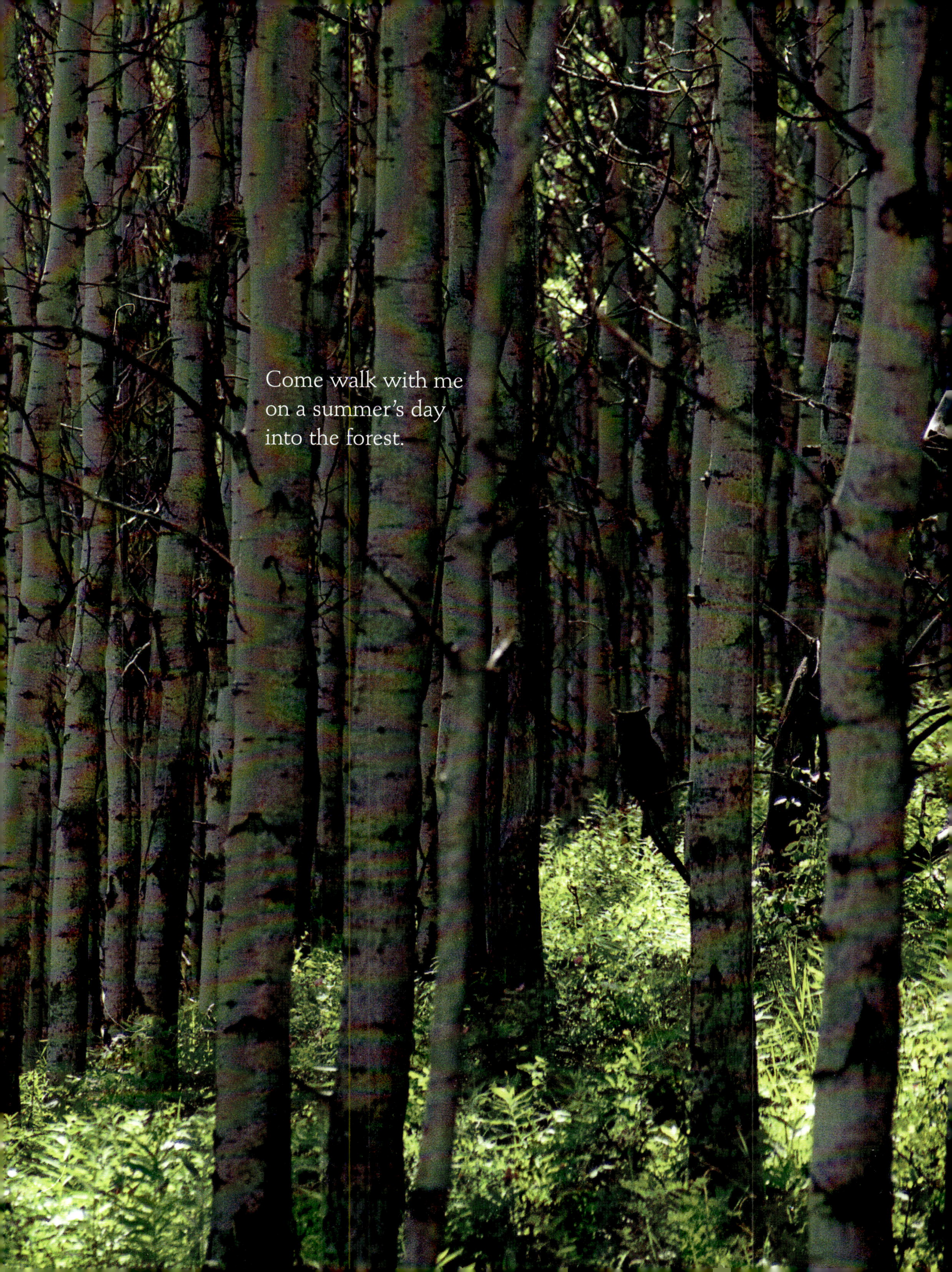

Come walk with me
on a summer's day
into the forest.

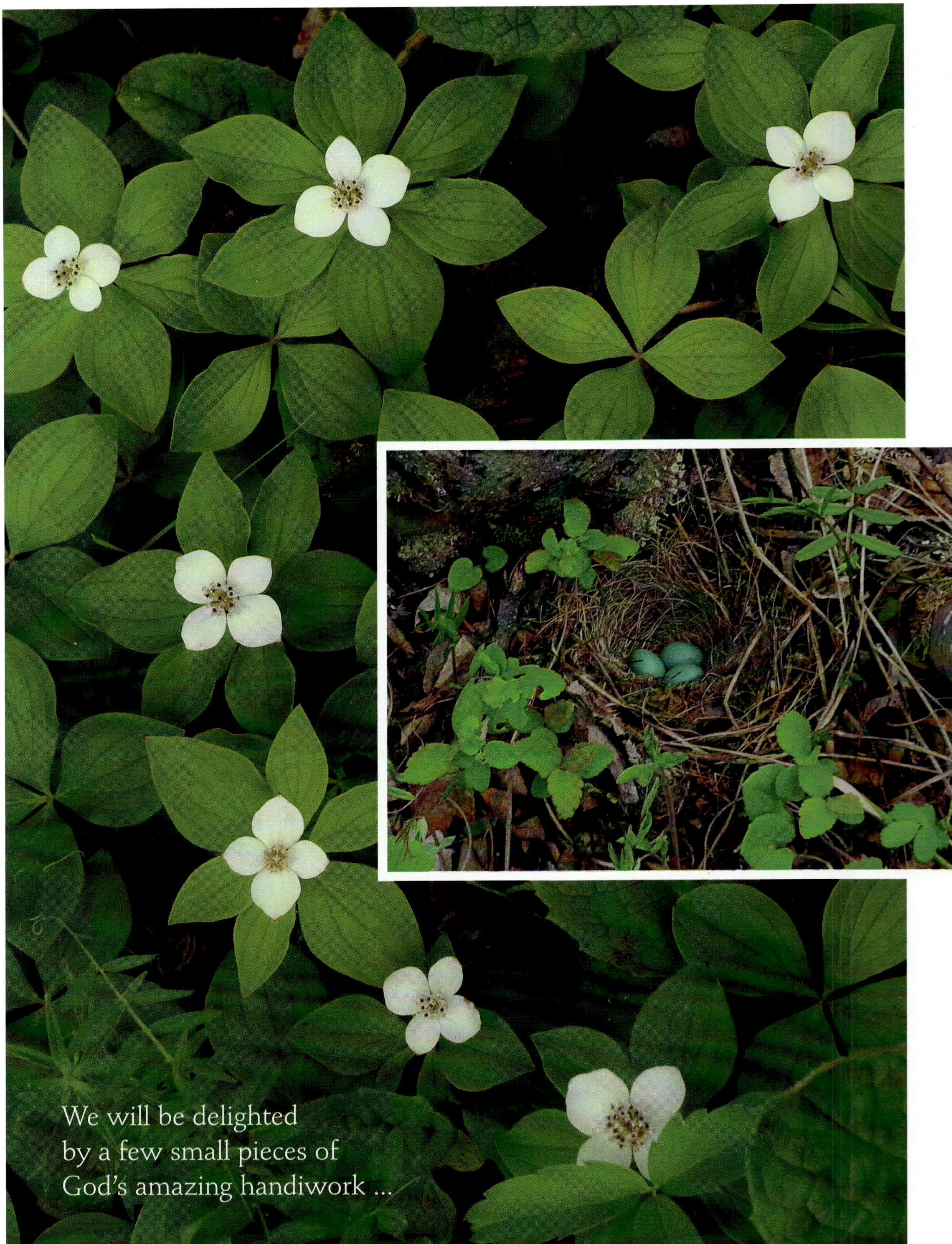

We will be delighted
by a few small pieces of
God's amazing handiwork ...

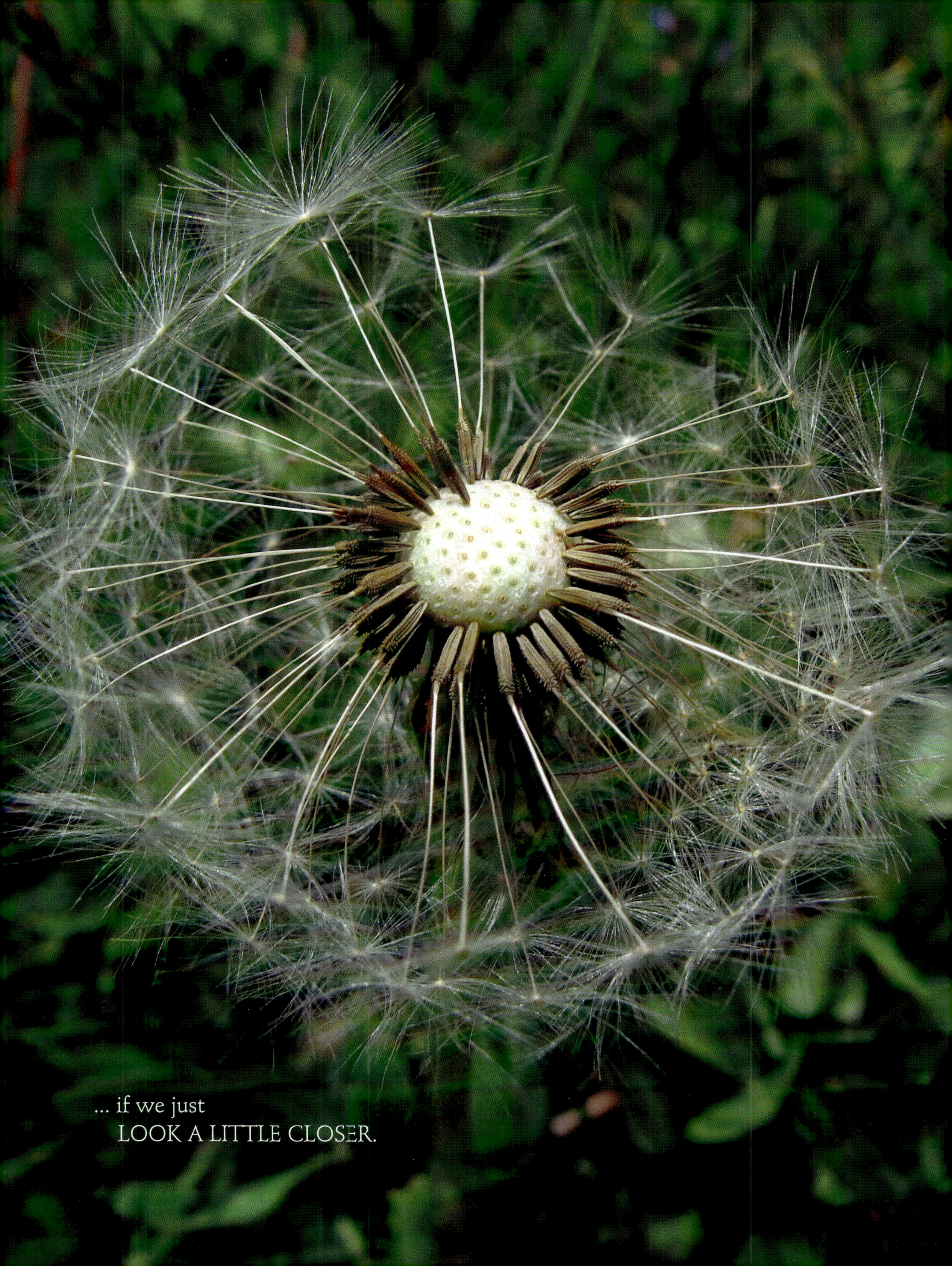

... if we just
LOOK A LITTLE CLOSER.

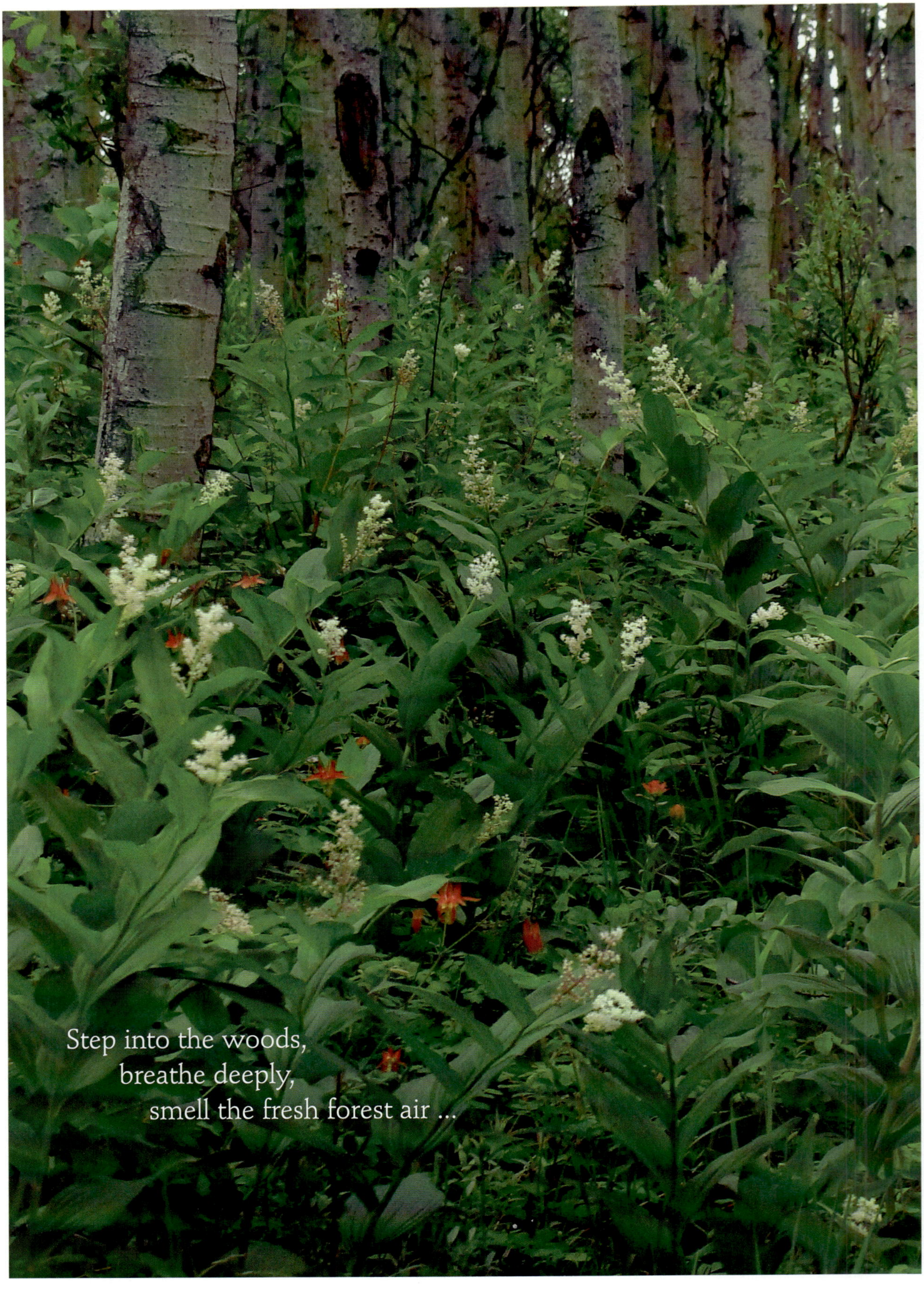
Step into the woods,
breathe deeply,
smell the fresh forest air ...

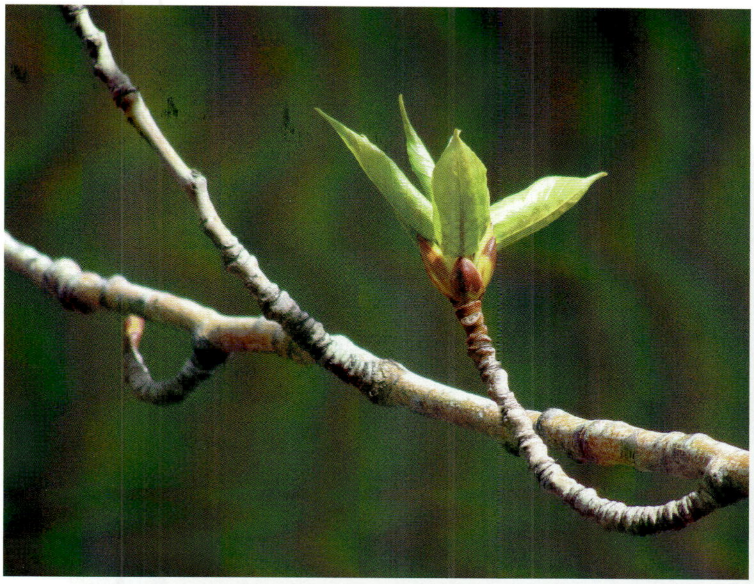

... and feel your burdens
begin to lift.

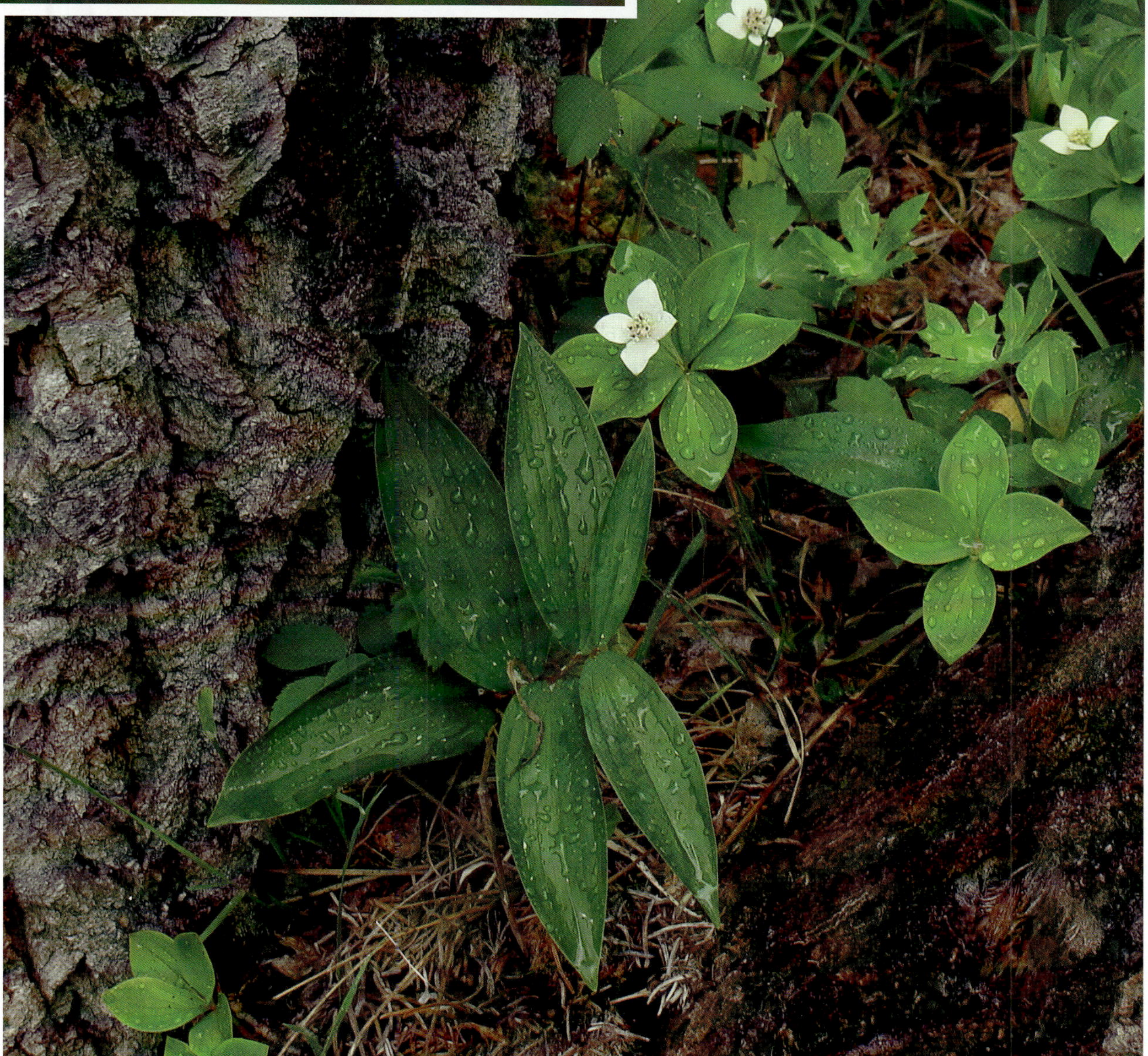

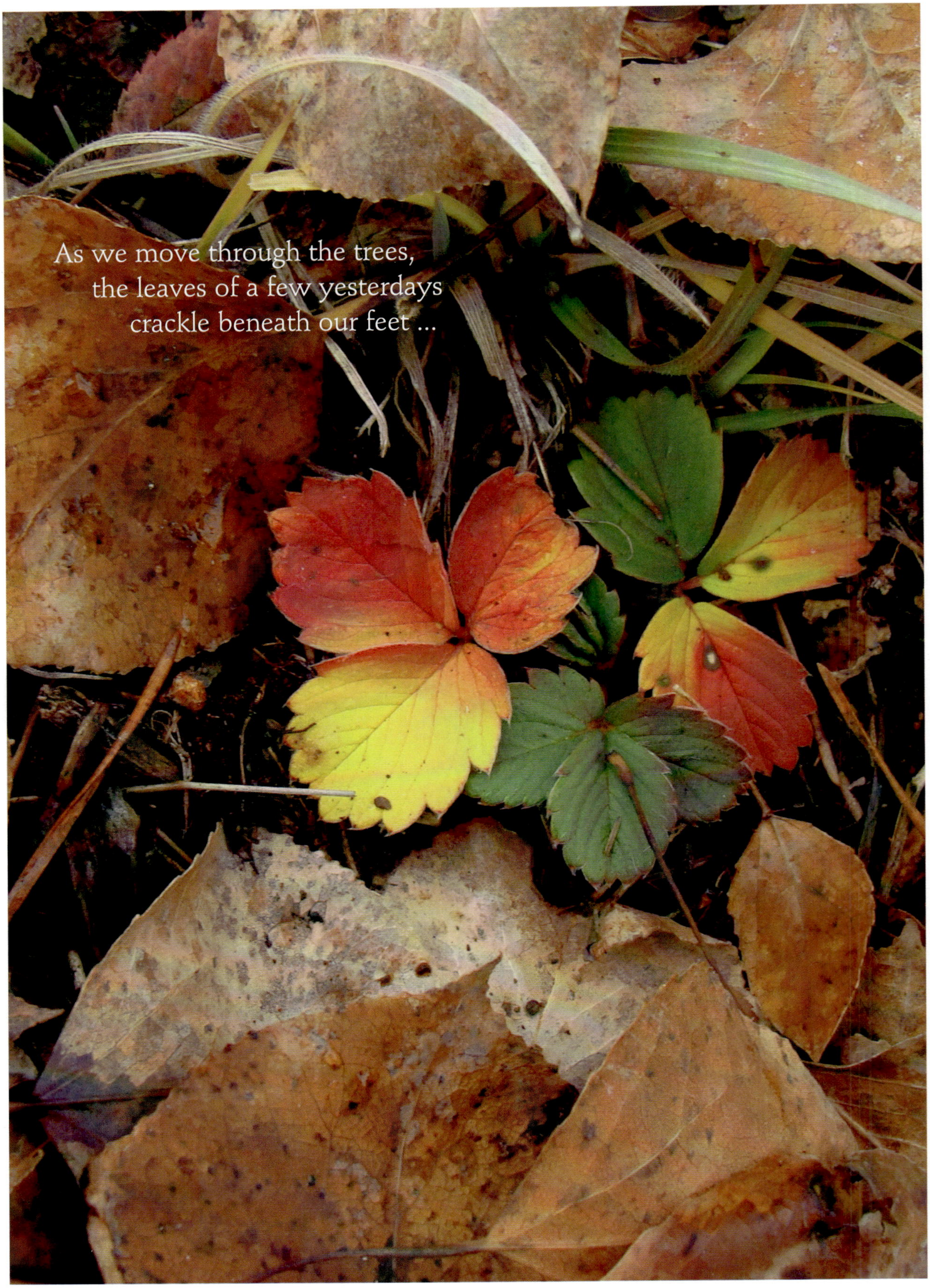

As we move through the trees,
the leaves of a few yesterdays
crackle beneath our feet ...

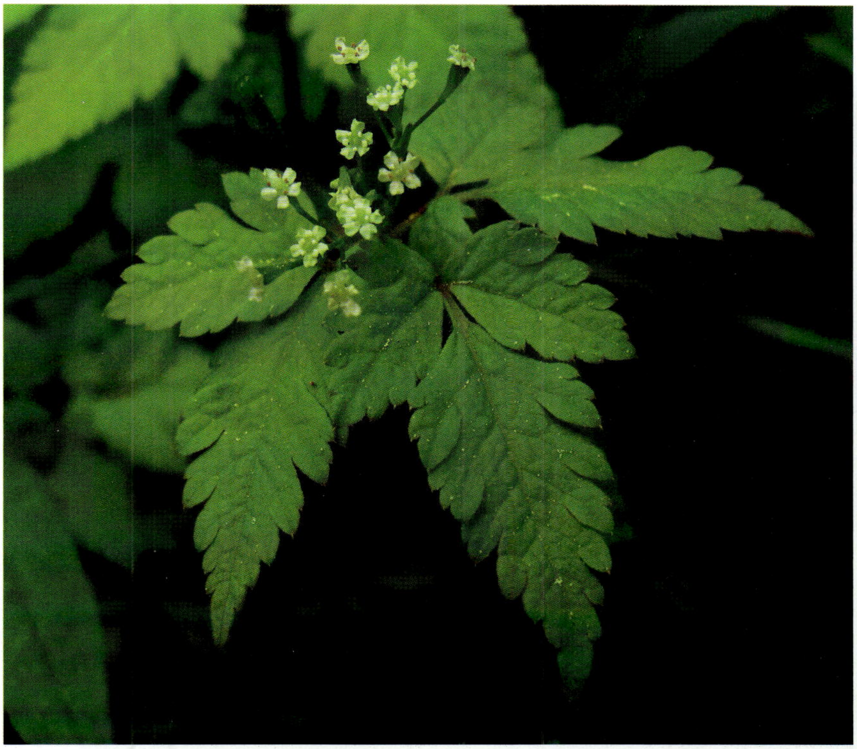

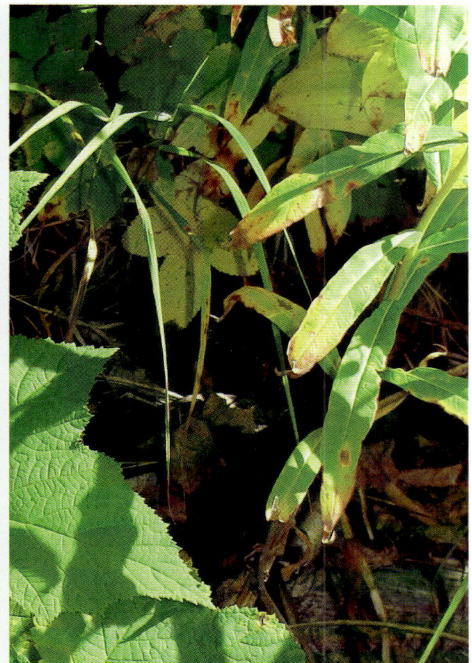

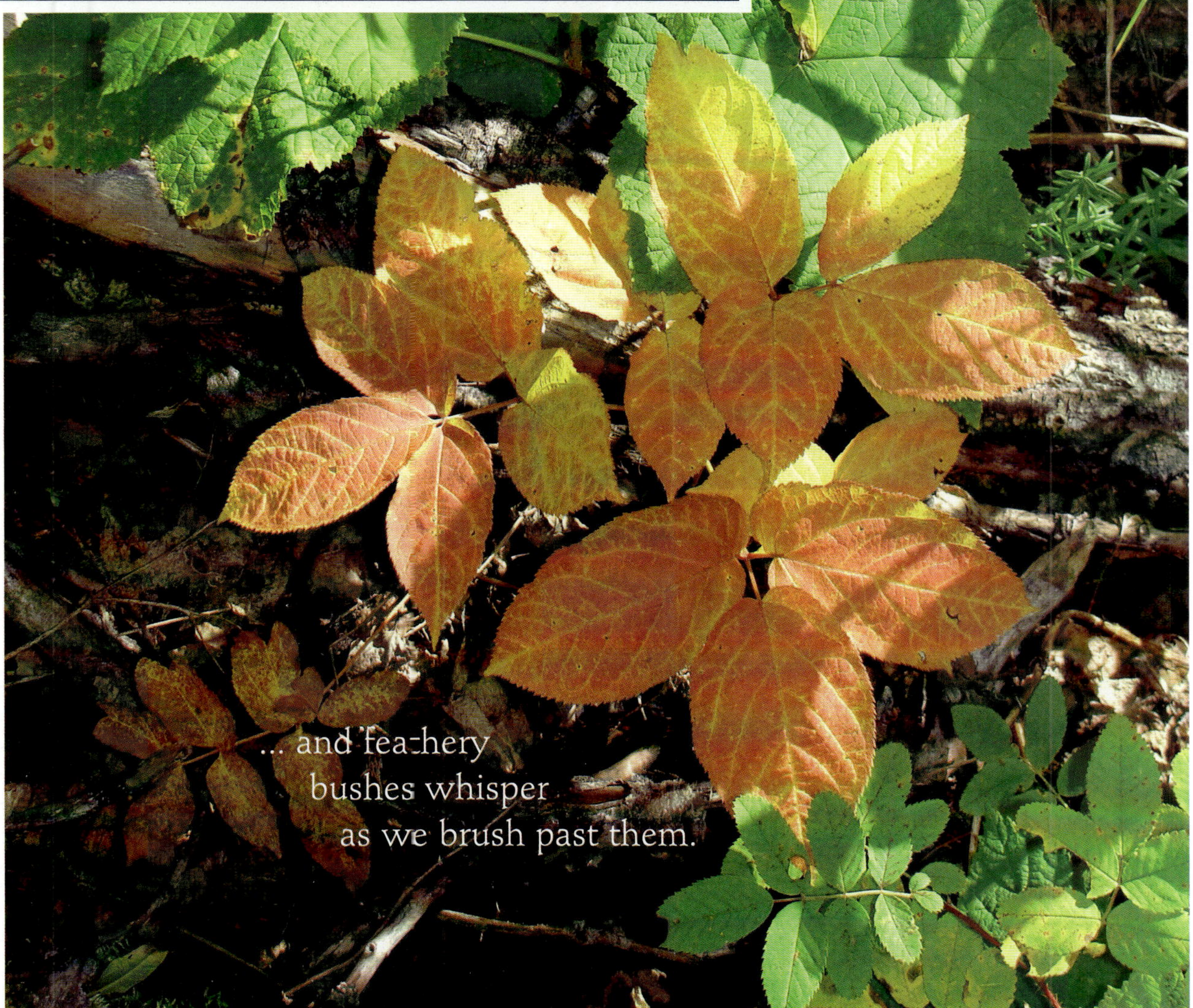

... and feathery
bushes whisper
as we brush past them.

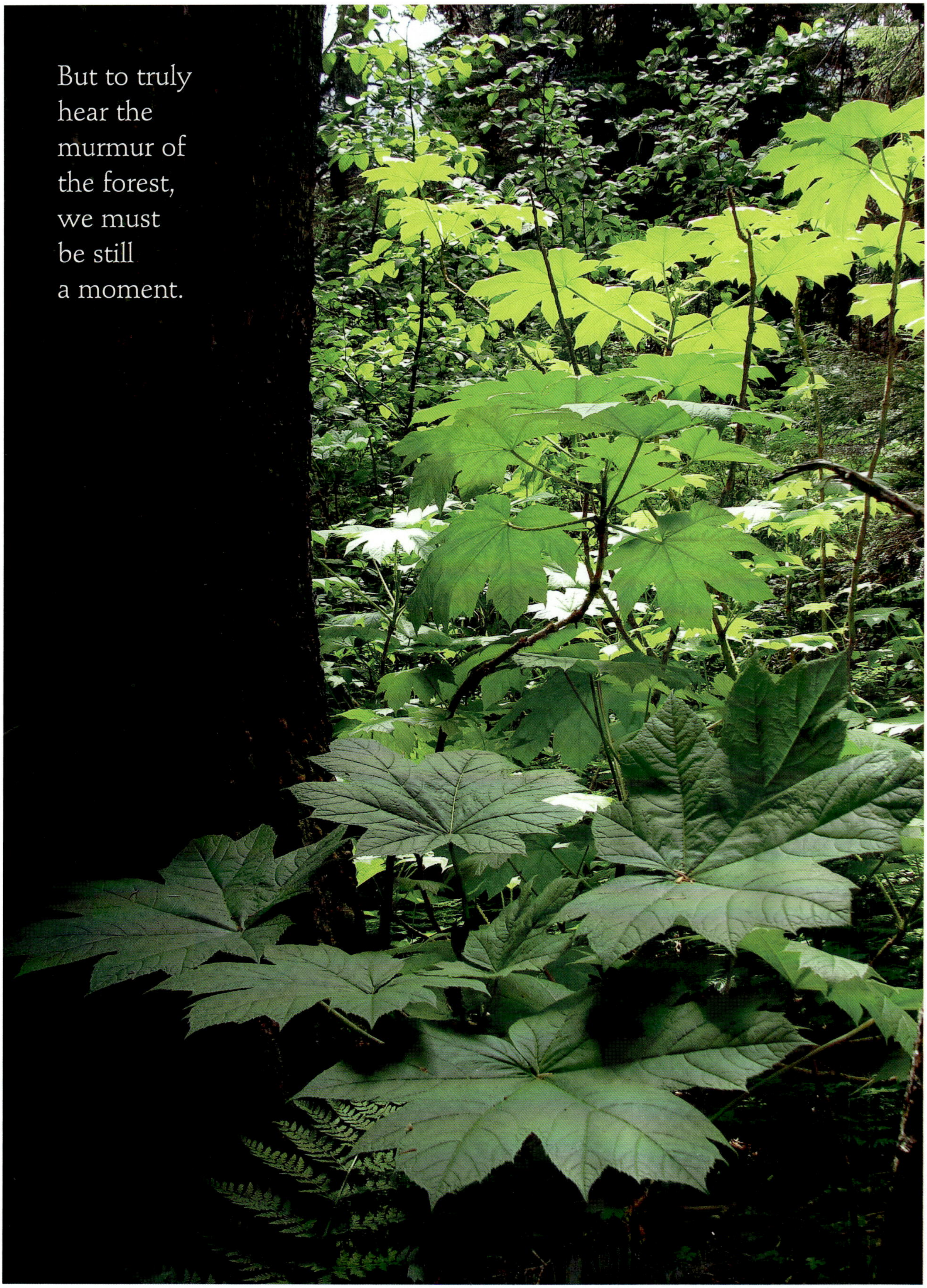

But to truly
hear the
murmur of
the forest,
we must
be still
a moment.

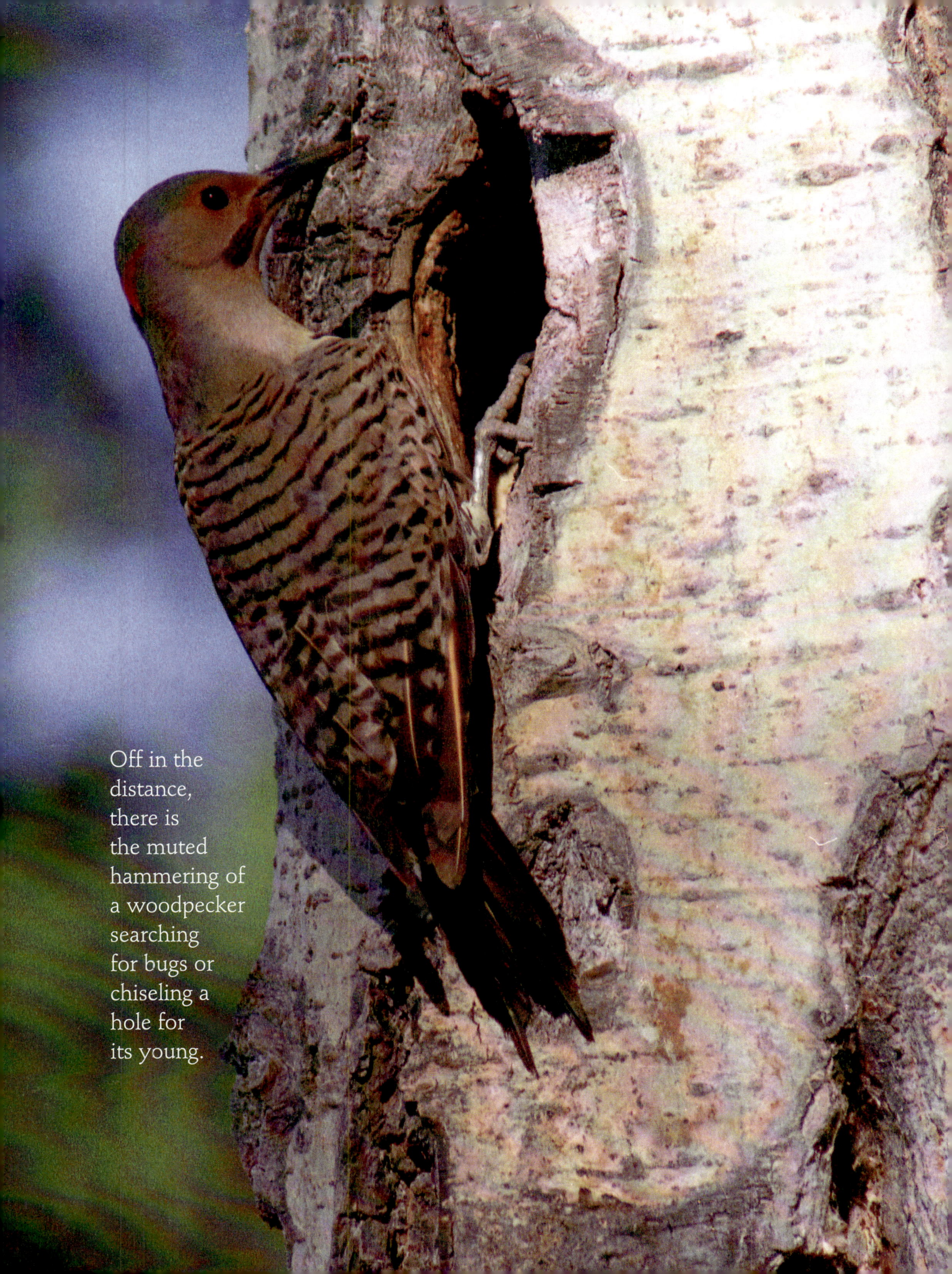

Off in the distance, there is the muted hammering of a woodpecker searching for bugs or chiseling a hole for its young.

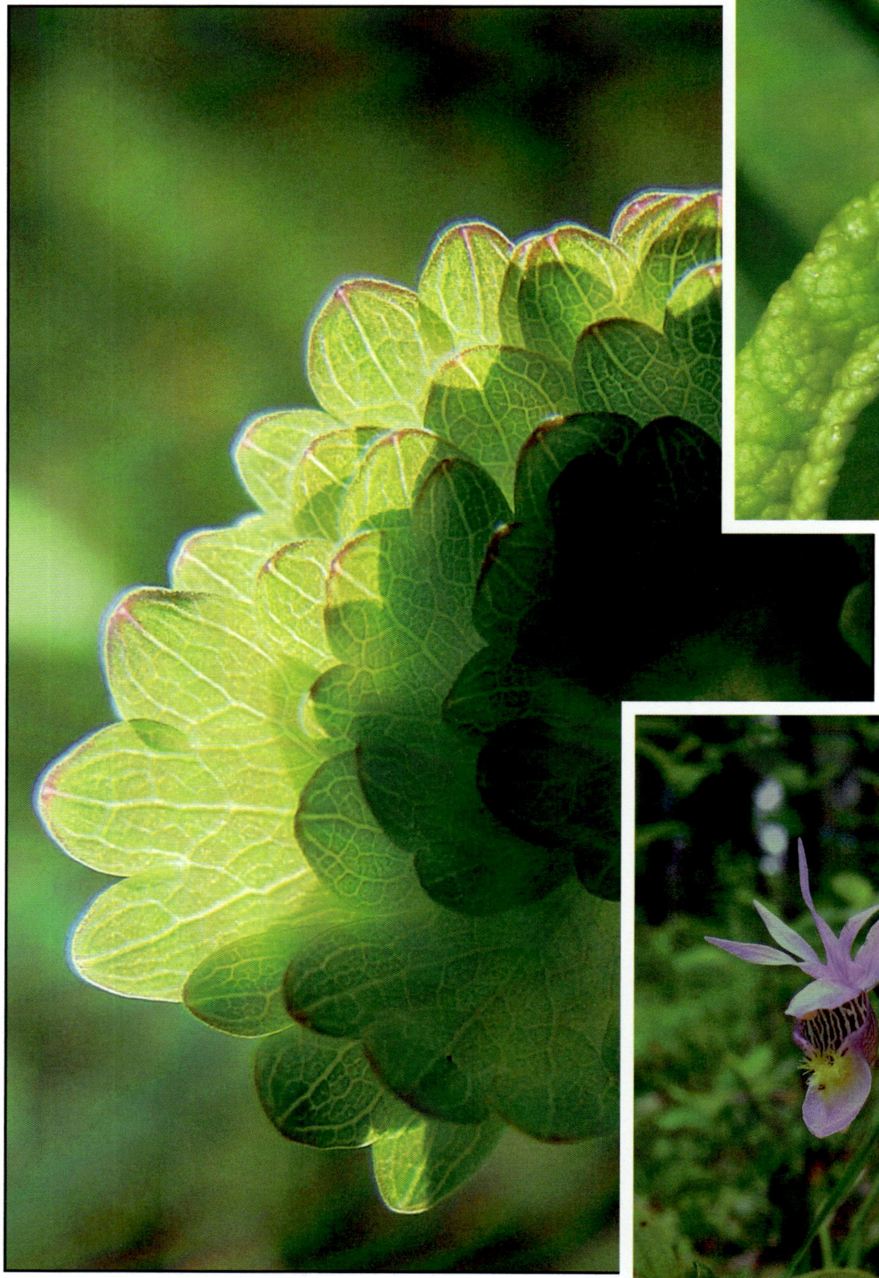

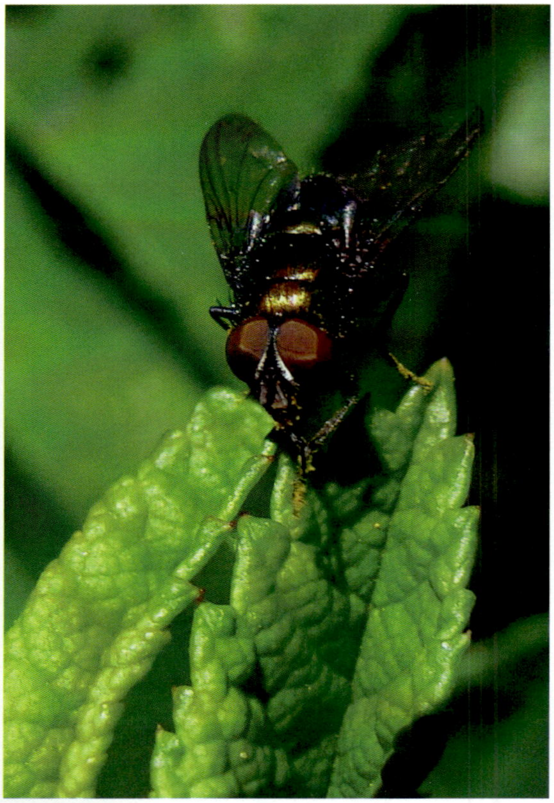

A fly
buzzes by
in the sun.

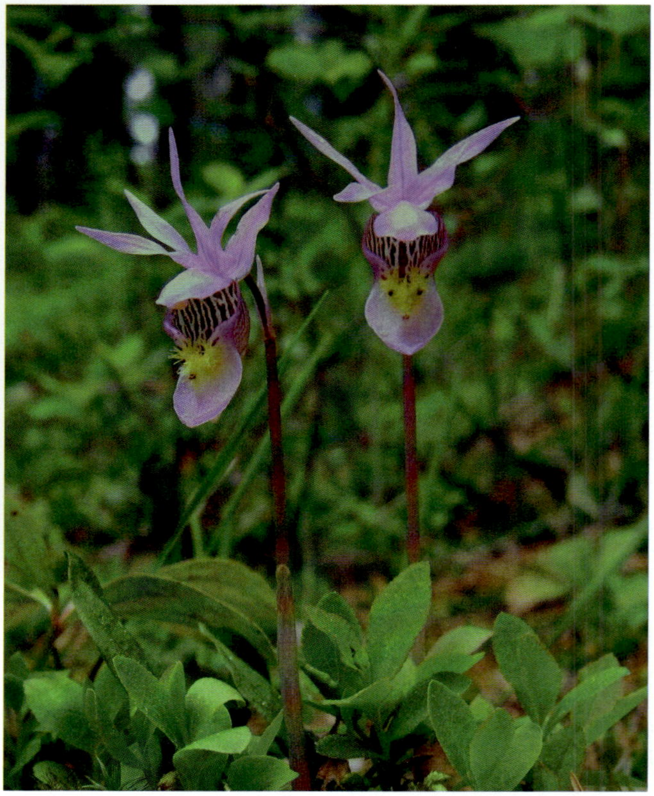

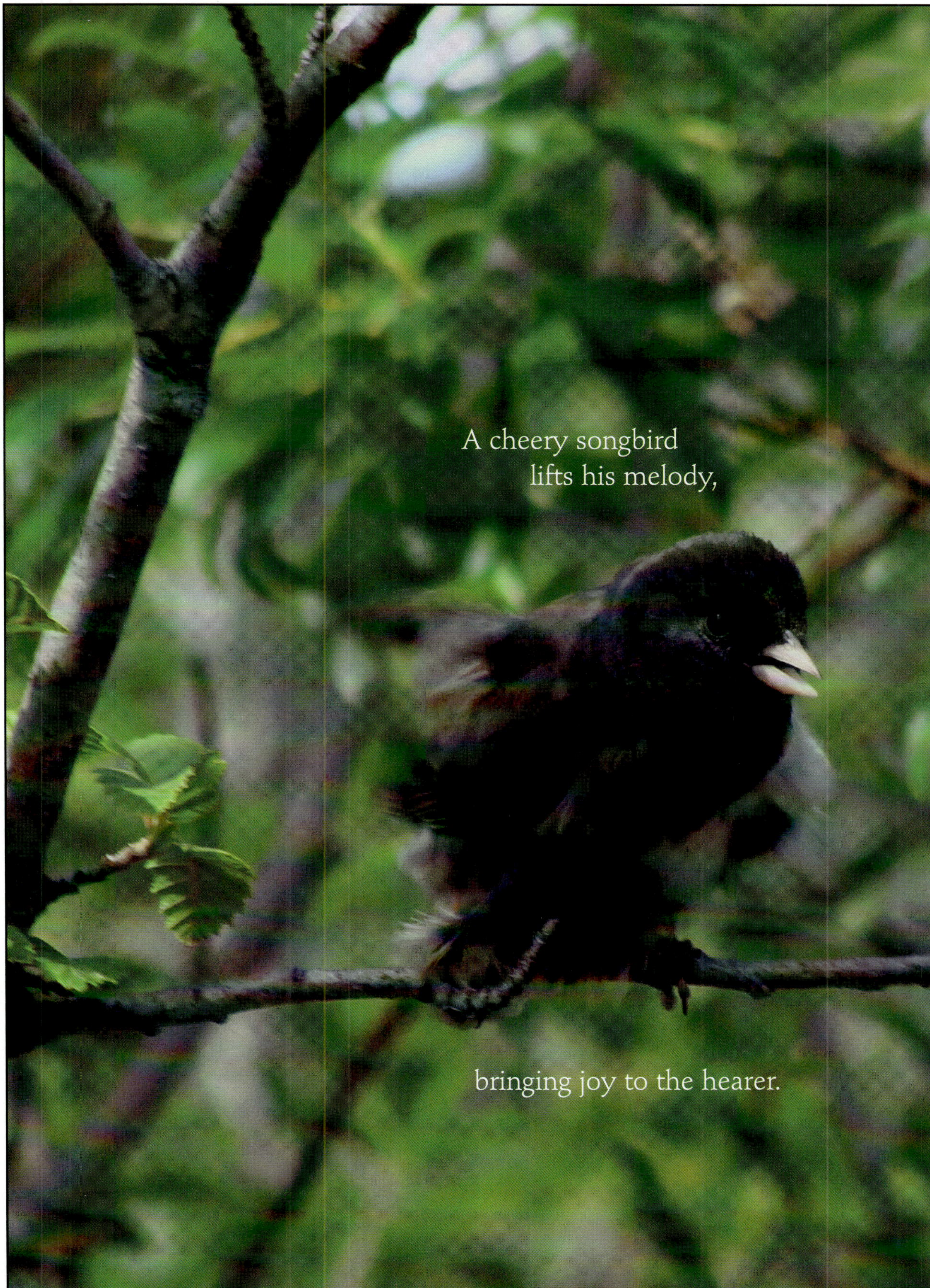

A cheery songbird
lifts his melody,

bringing joy to the hearer.

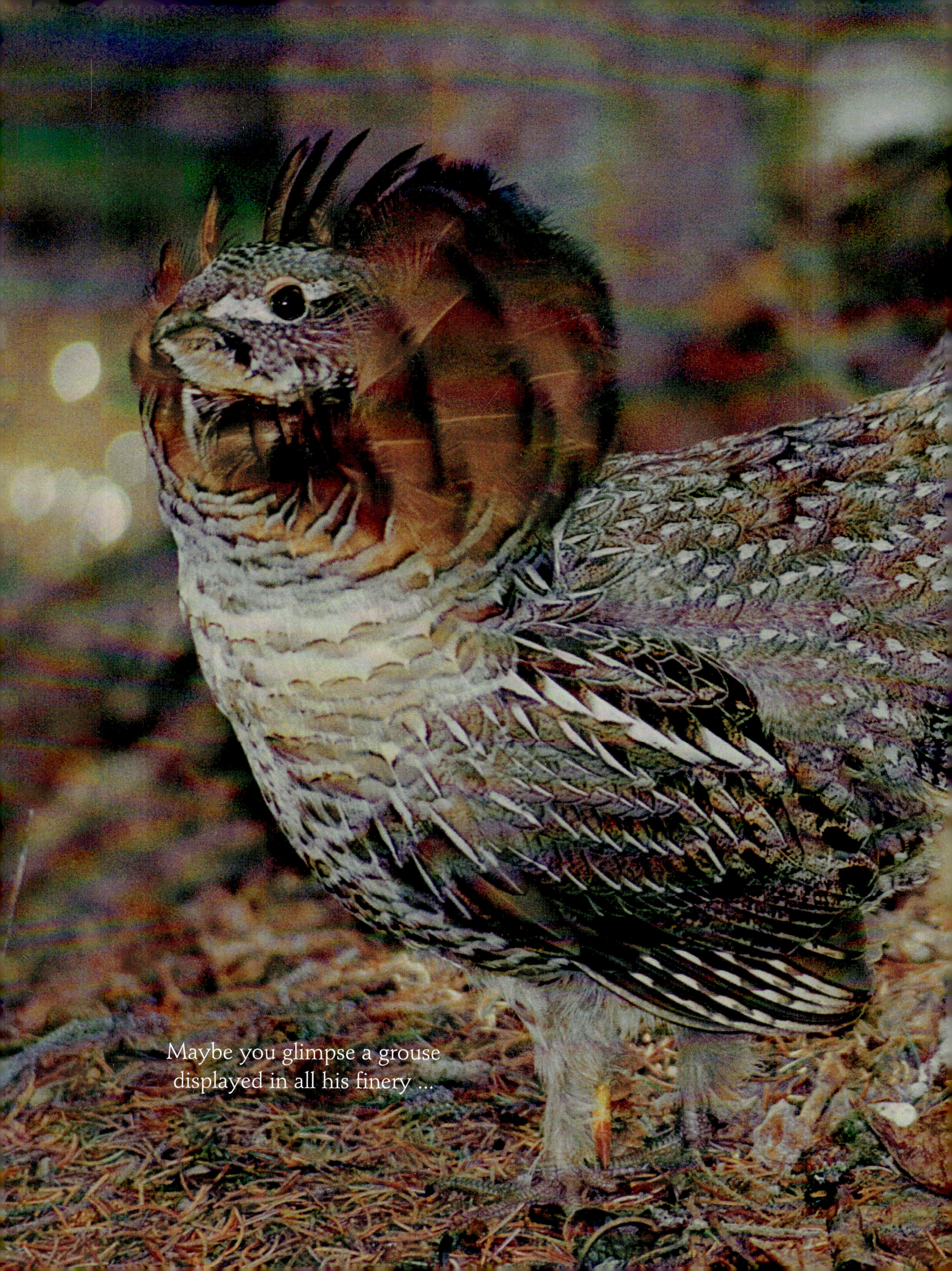

Maybe you glimpse a grouse
displayed in all his finery ...

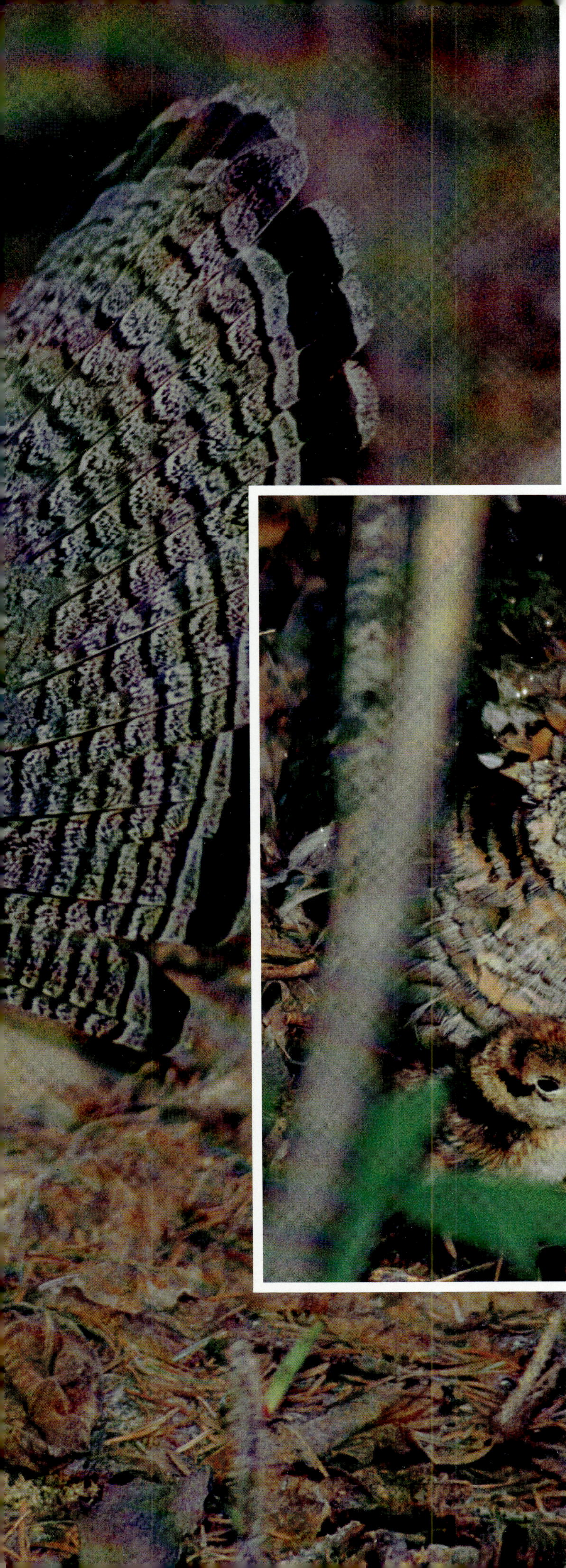

... or secretly camouflaged
on a nest on the forest floor.

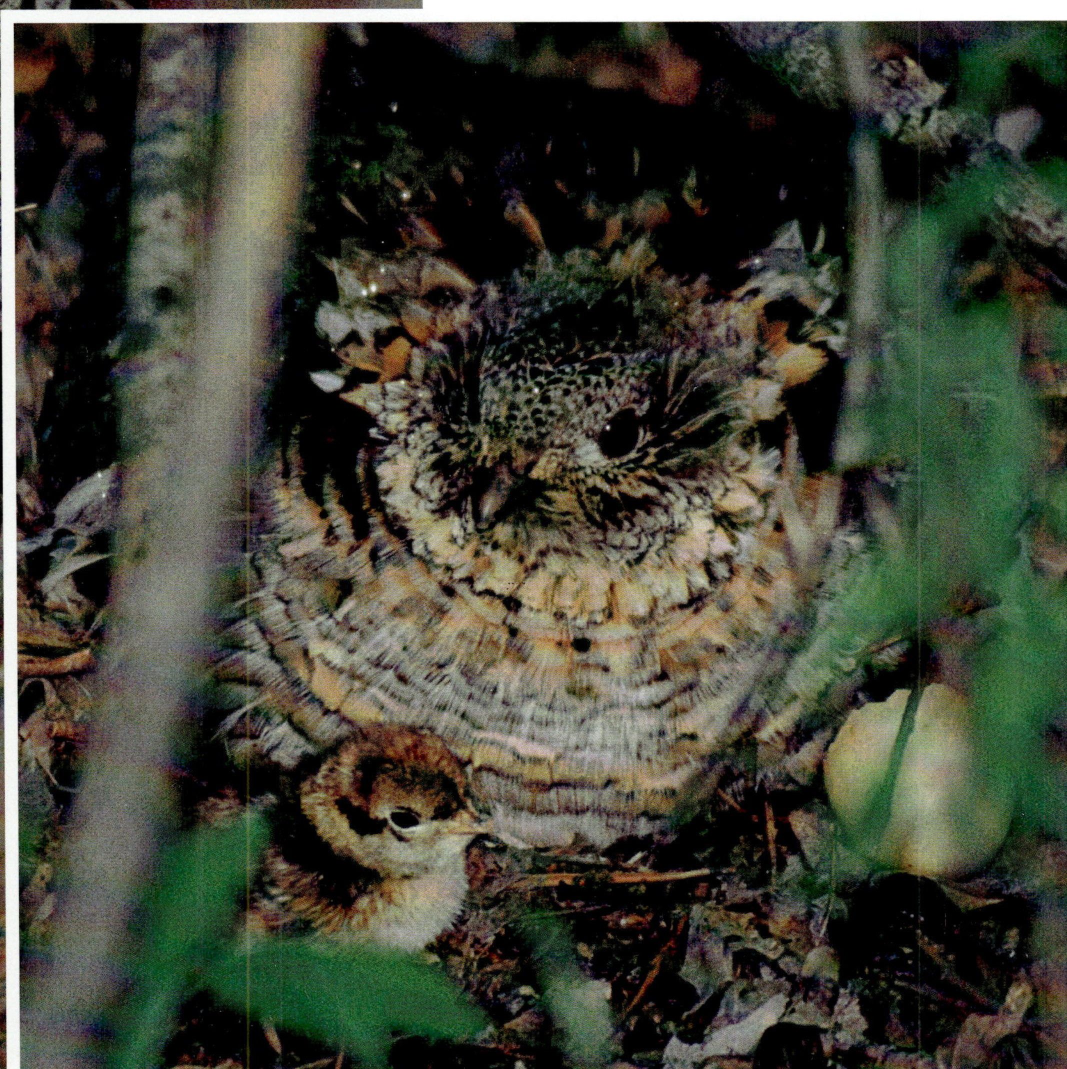

Its markings blend
so beautifully with
the surroundings.

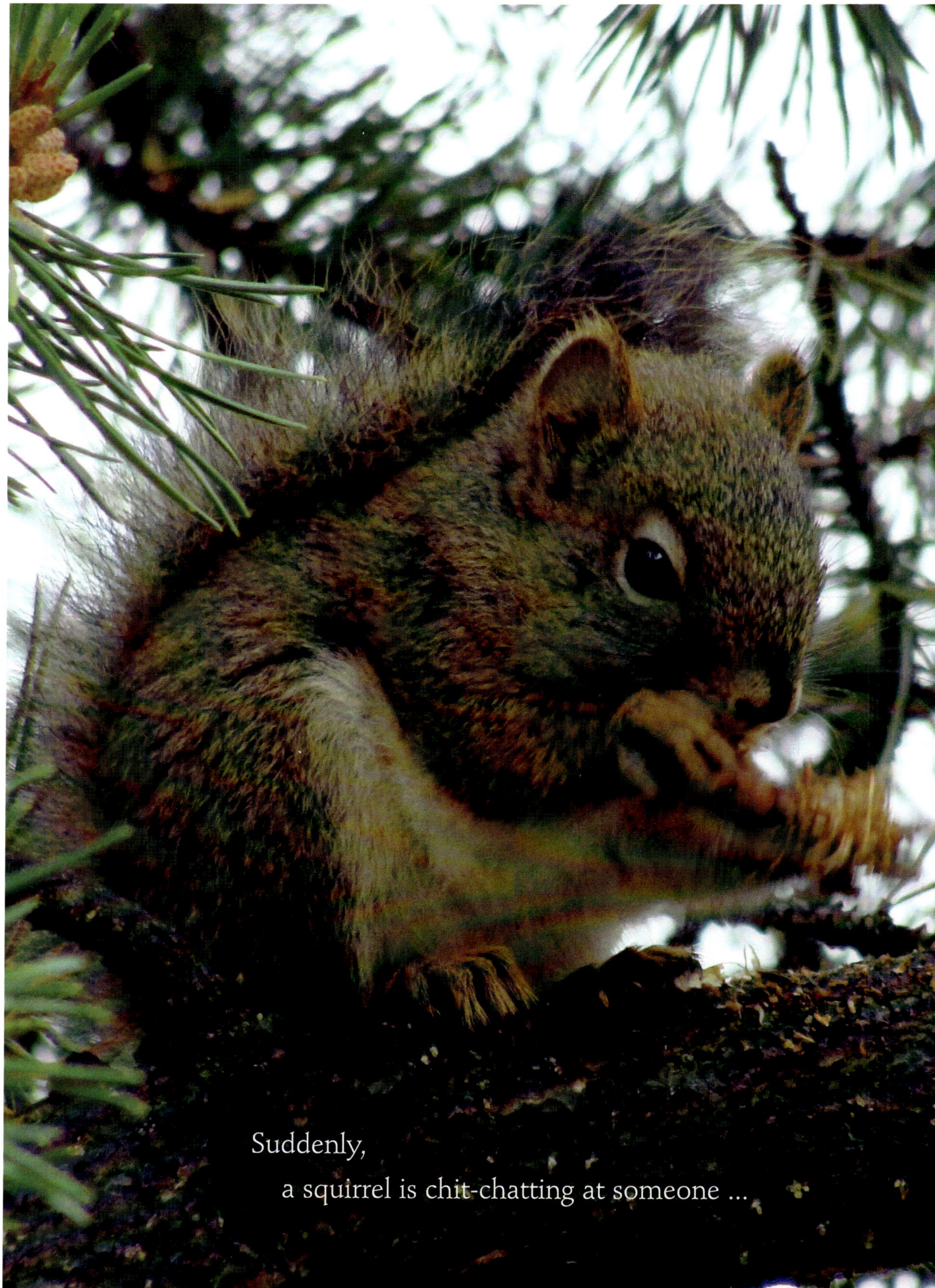

Suddenly,
a squirrel is chit-chatting at someone ...

... or something
that cares to
annoy him.

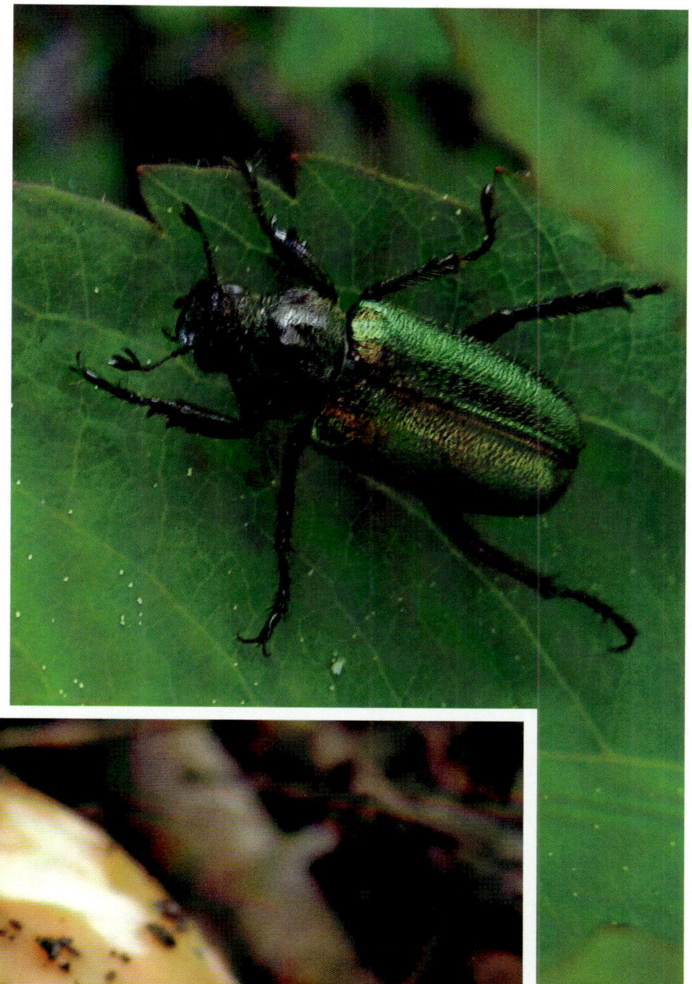

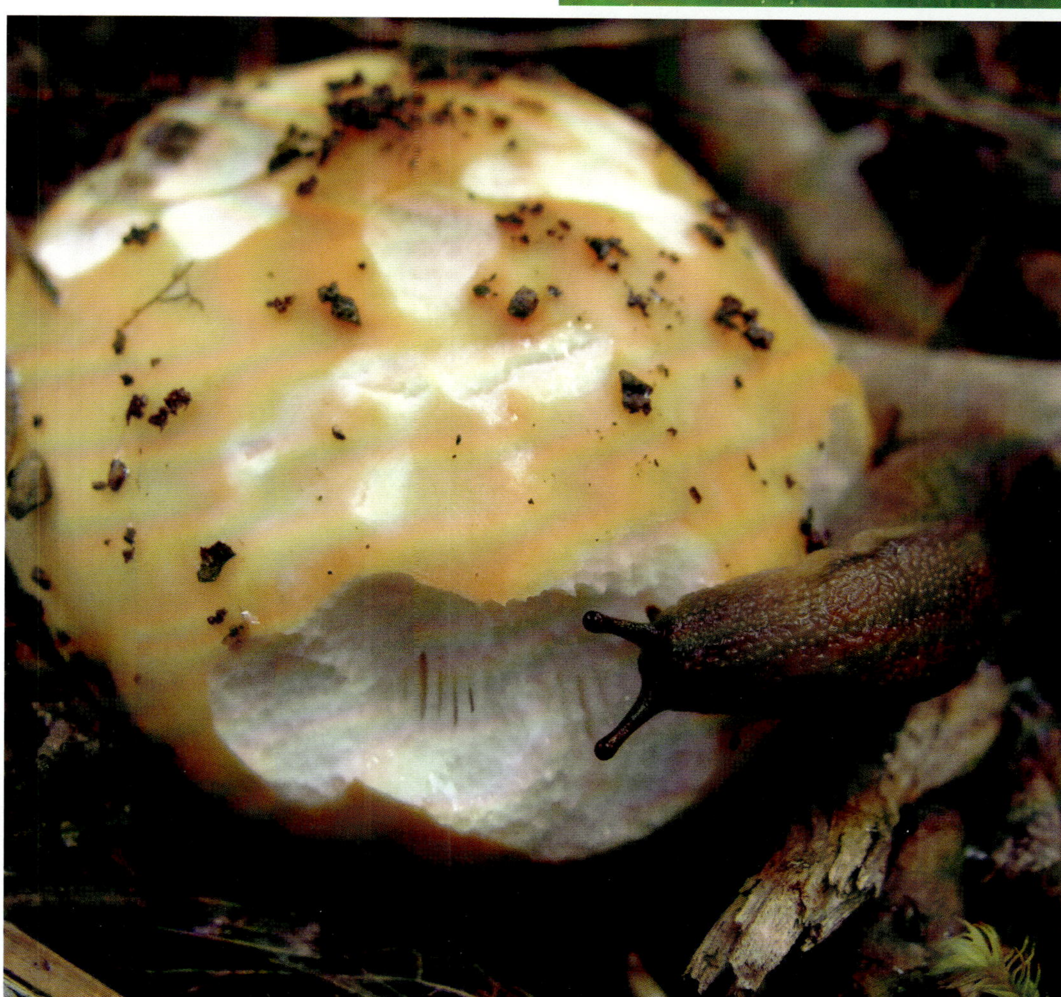

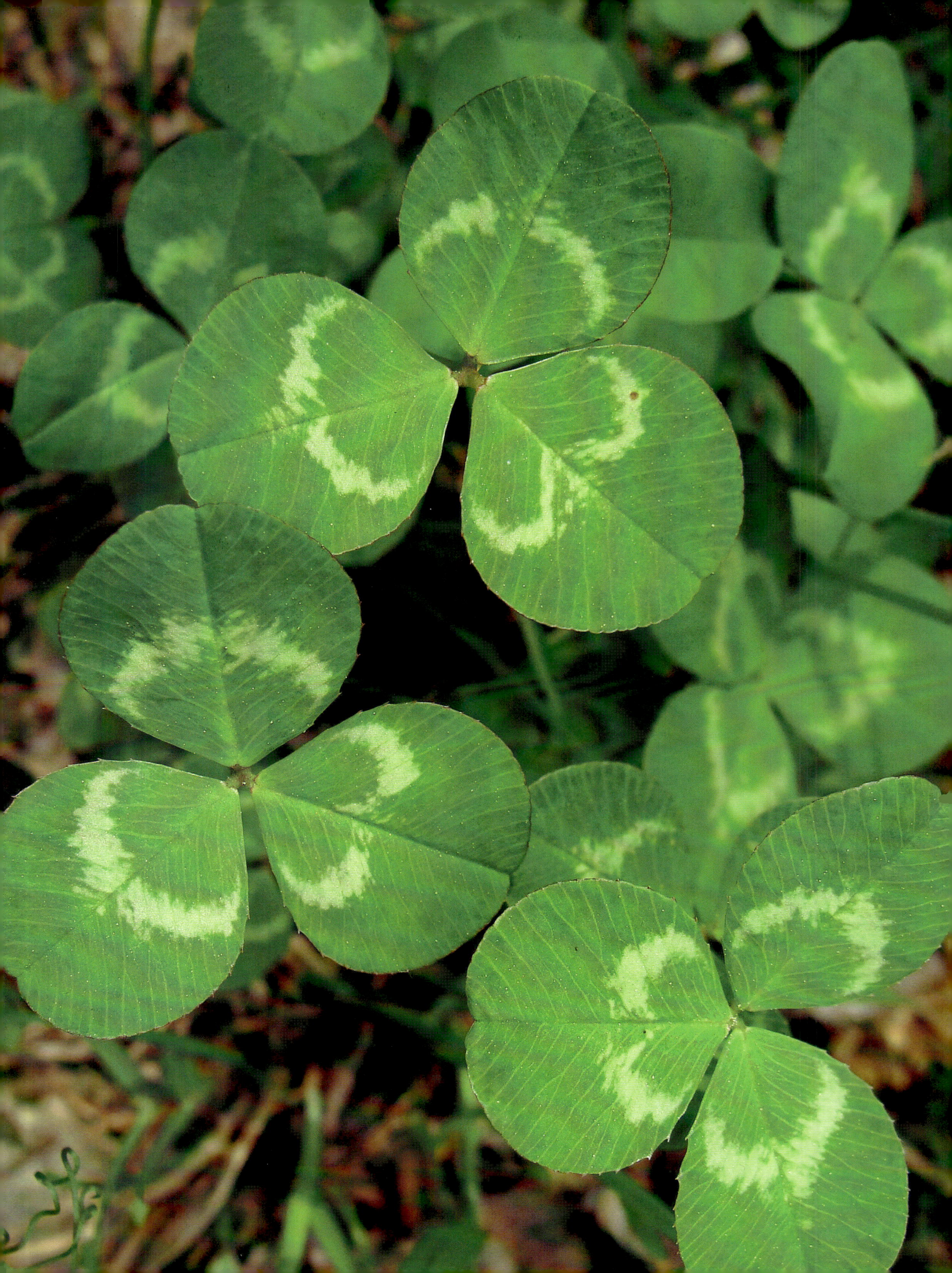

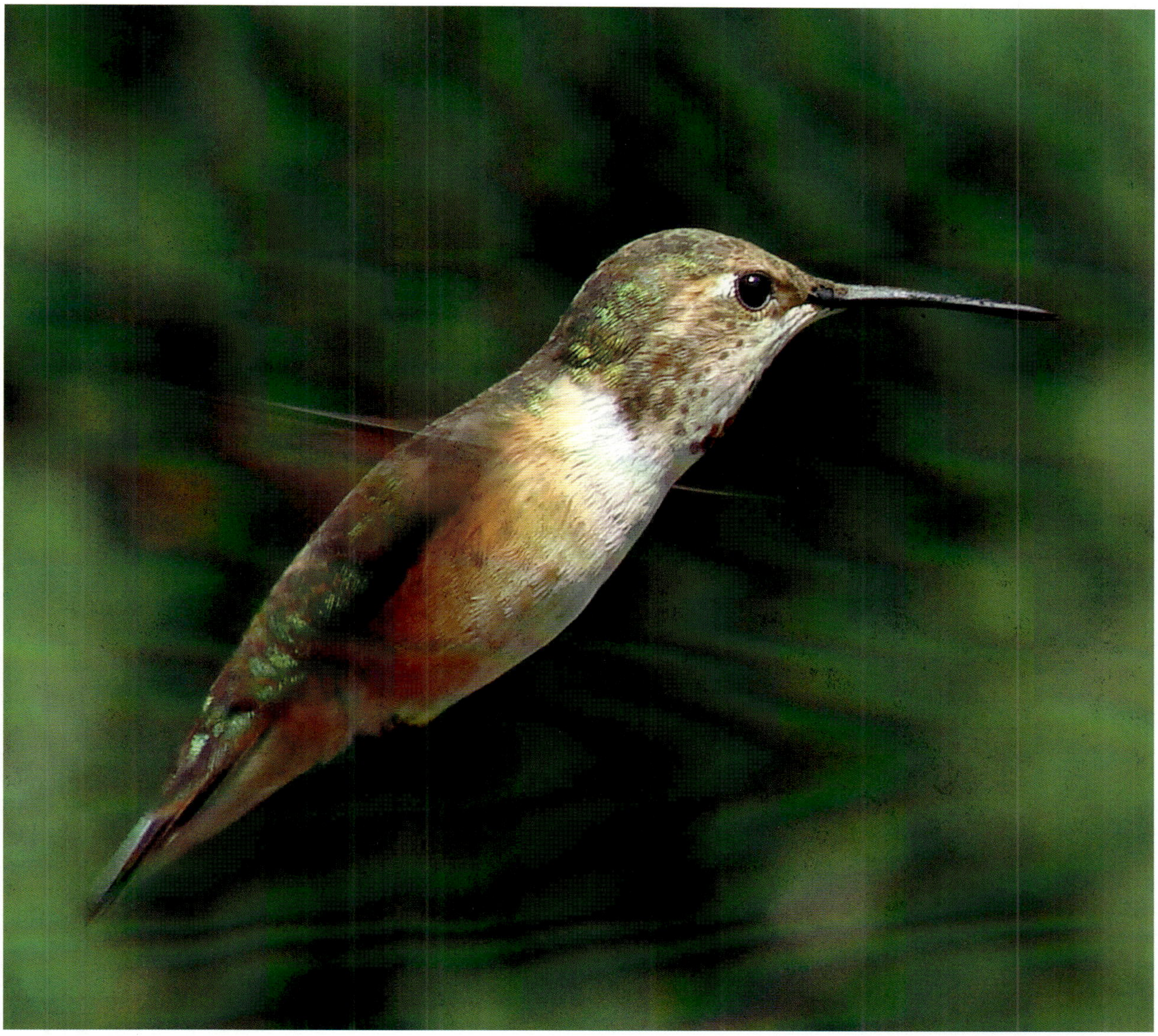

The attentive observer finds delight in both
the sights and sounds of the woodland.

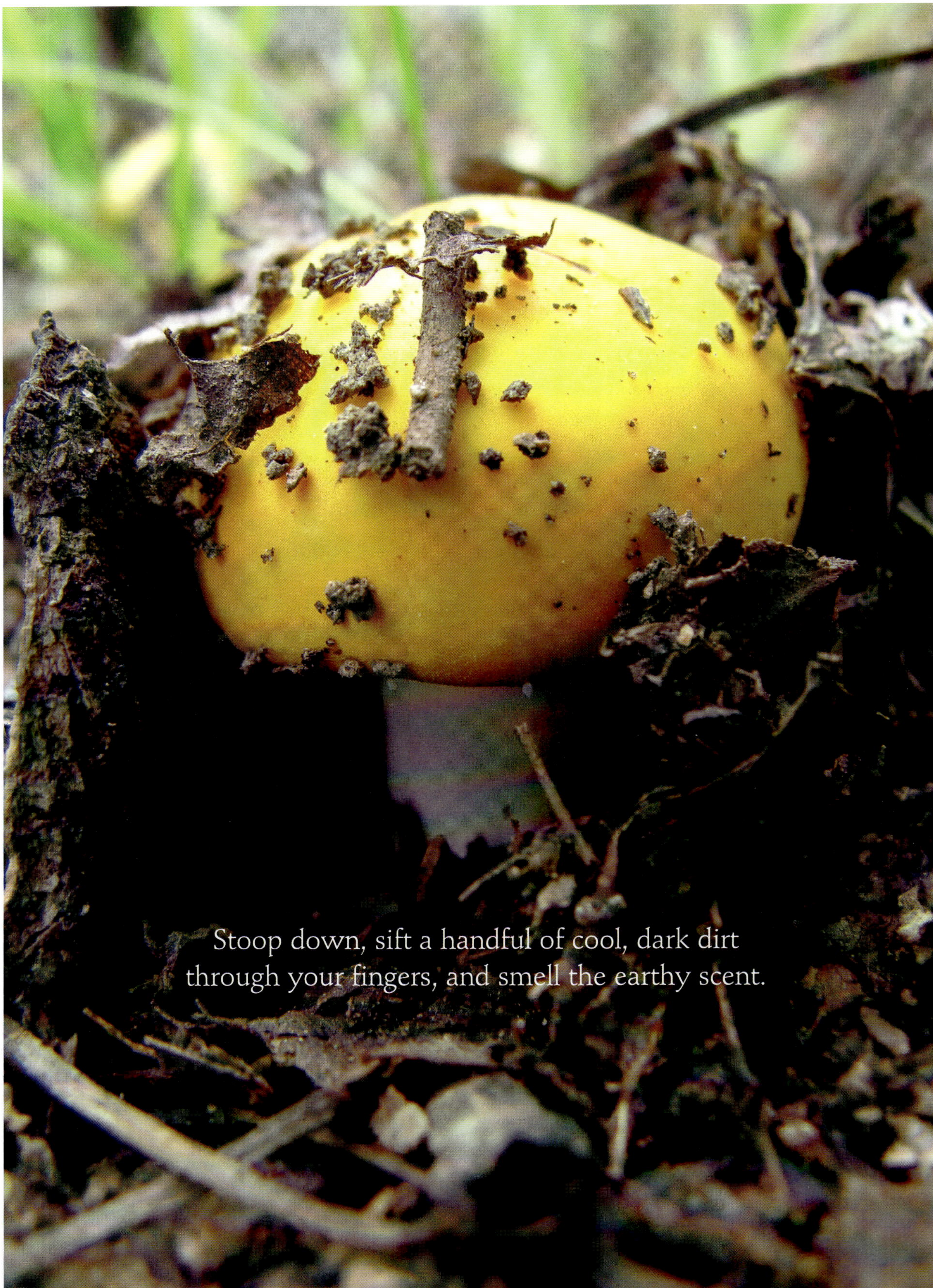

Stoop down, sift a handful of cool, dark dirt through your fingers, and smell the earthy scent.

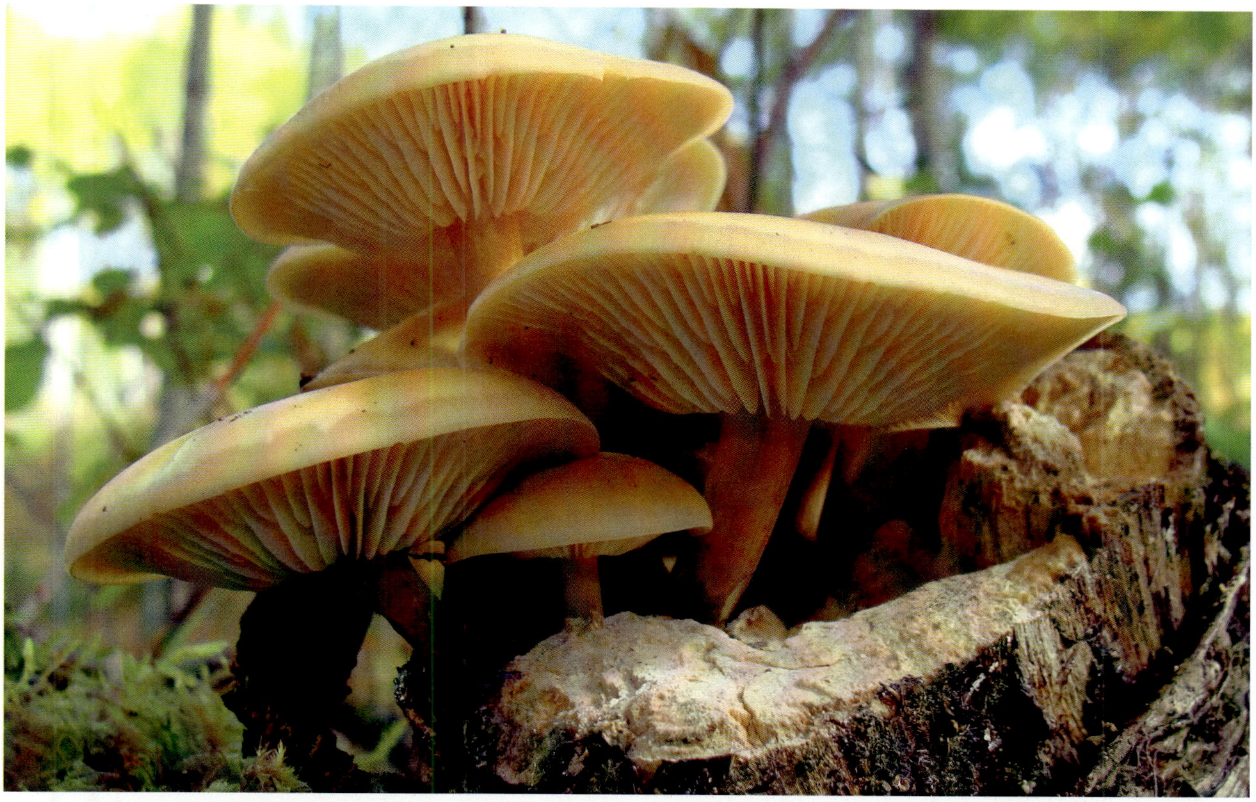

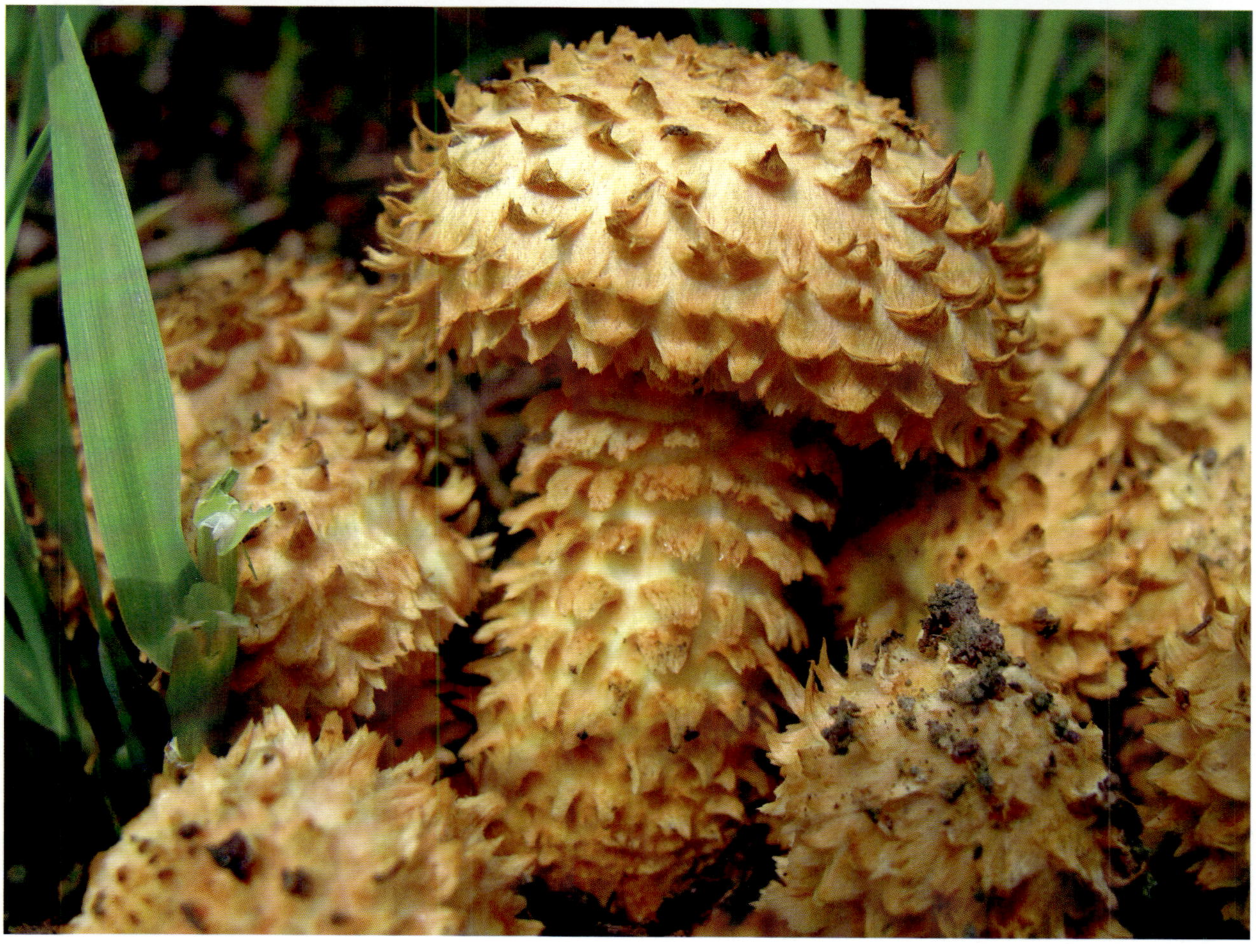

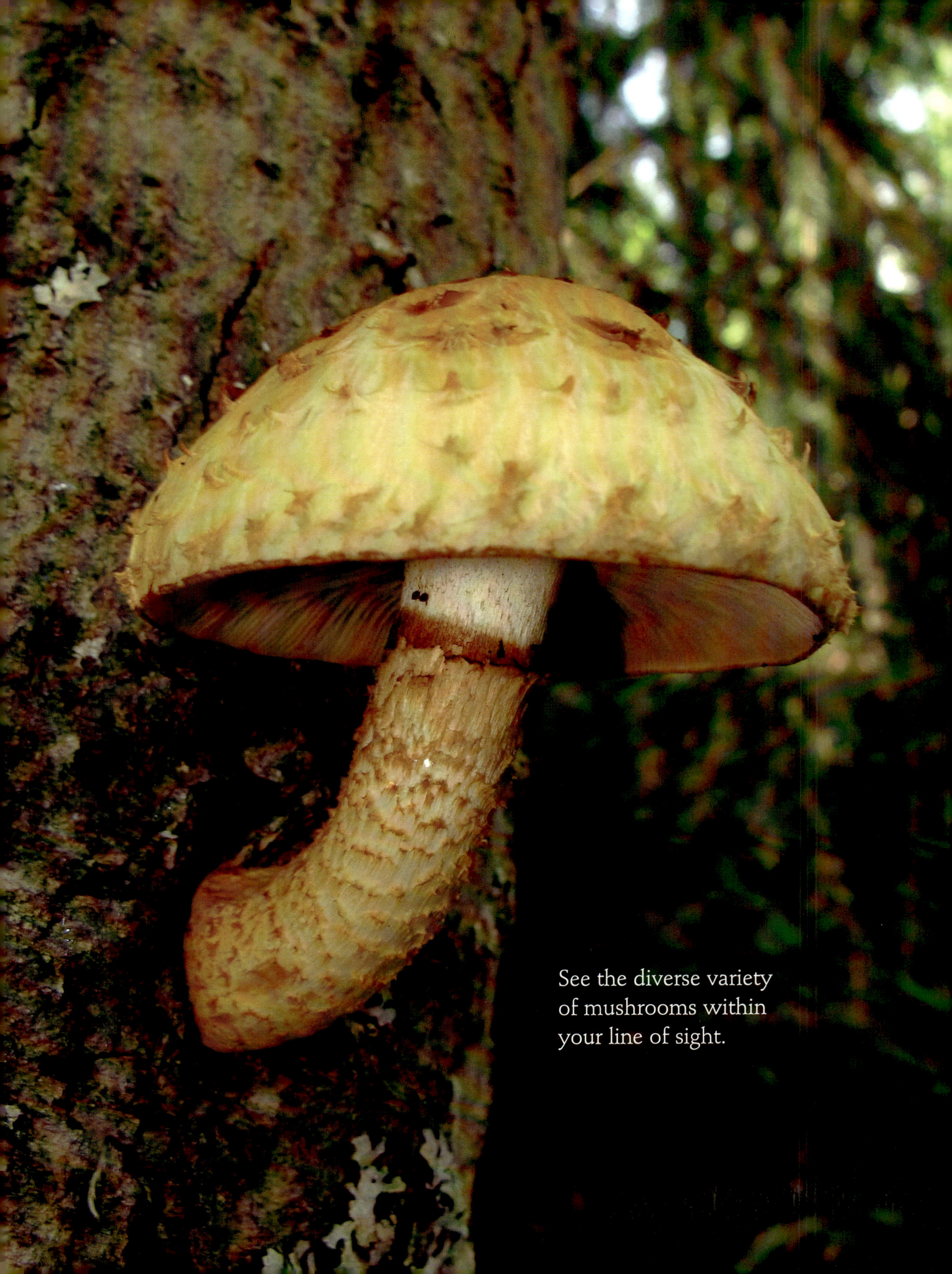

See the diverse variety of mushrooms within your line of sight.

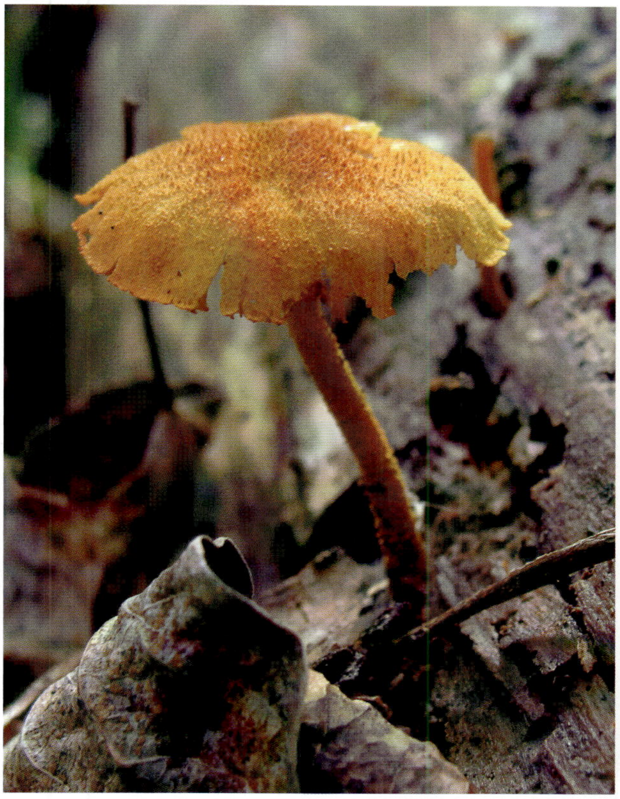

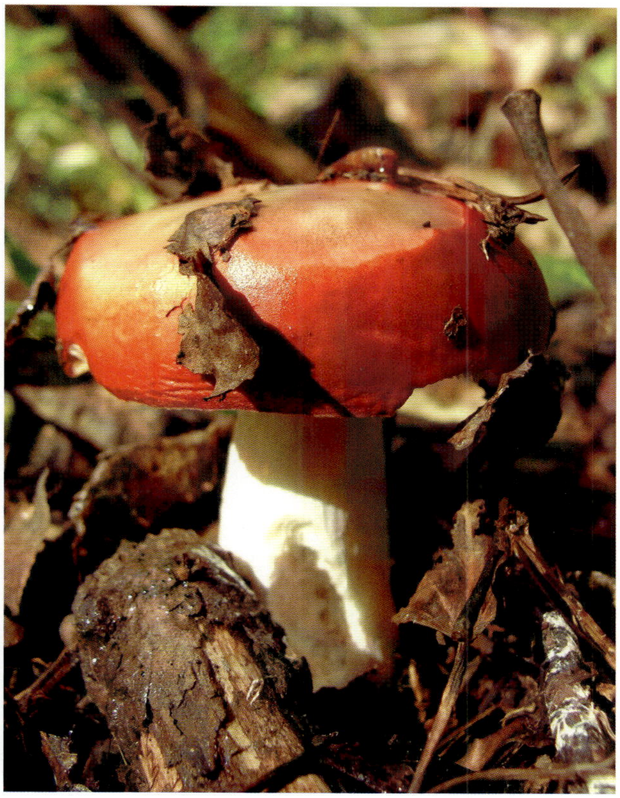

Are they not amazing?

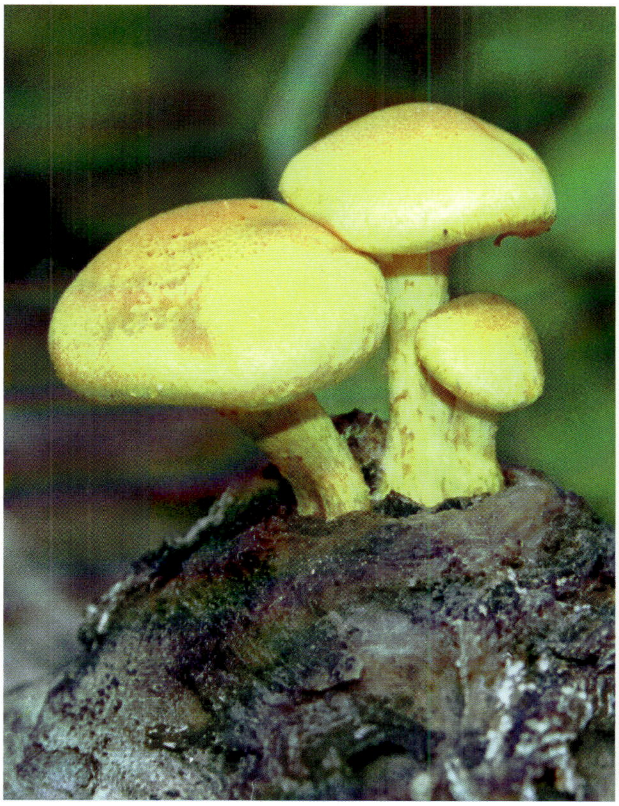

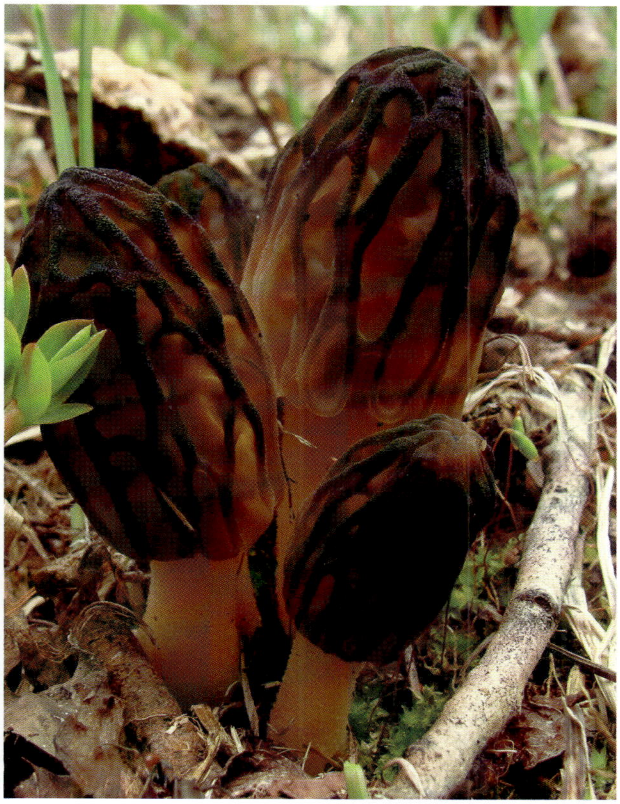

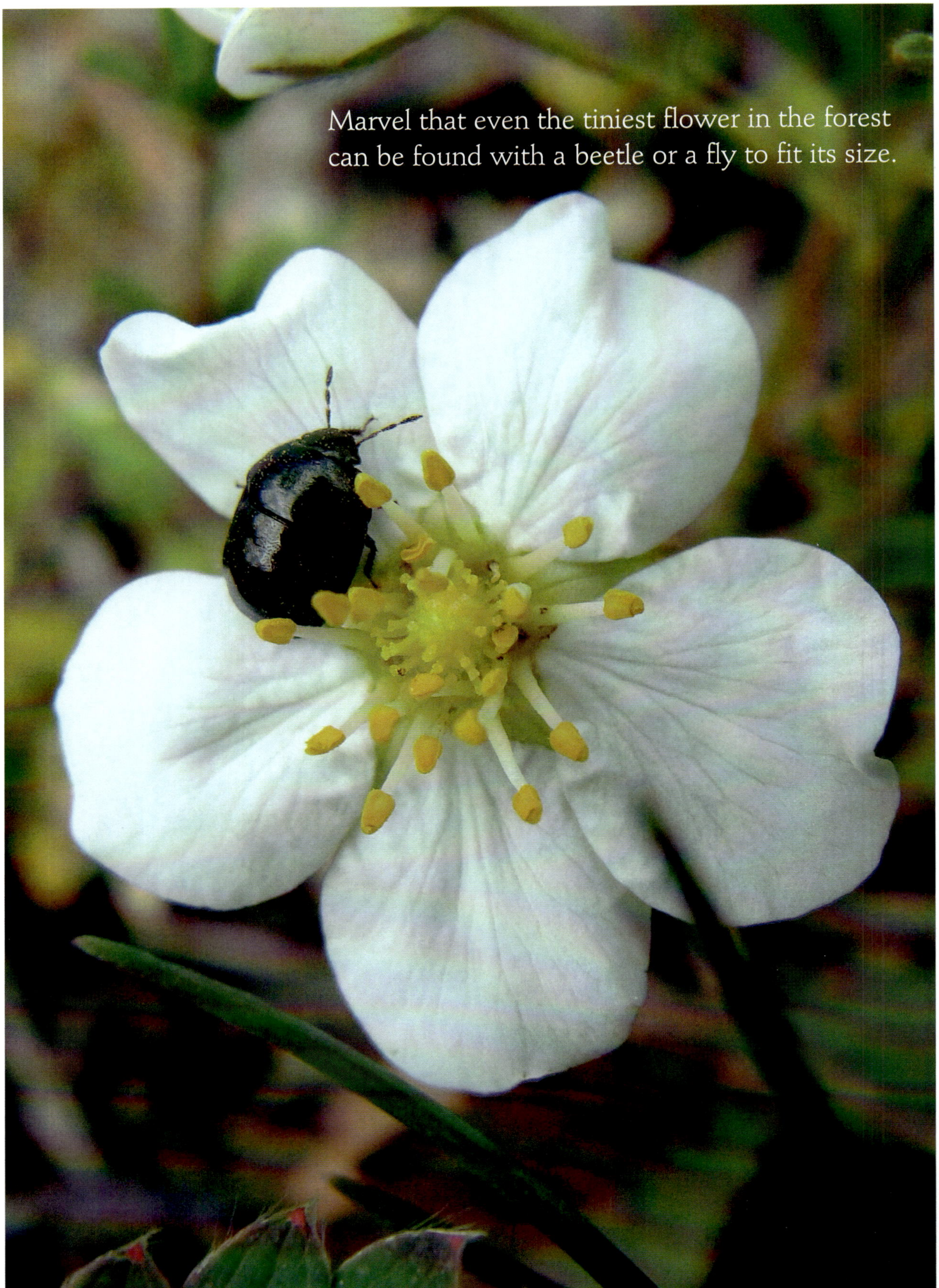
Marvel that even the tiniest flower in the forest
can be found with a beetle or a fly to fit its size.

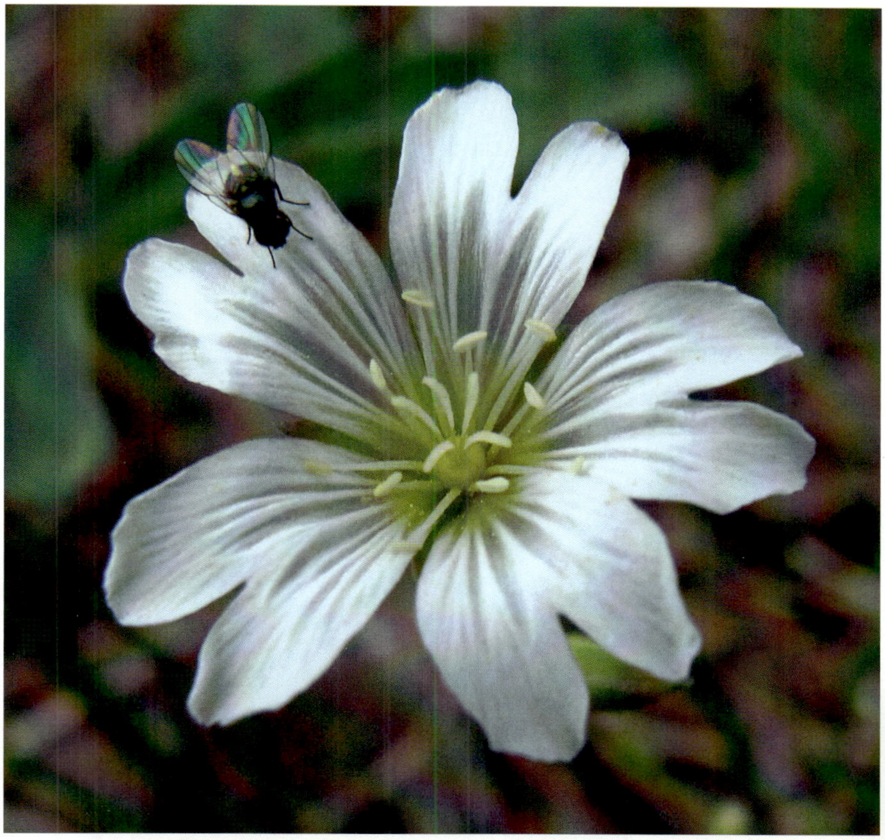

And see the tiny snails feeding on the sap of a fallen pinecone.

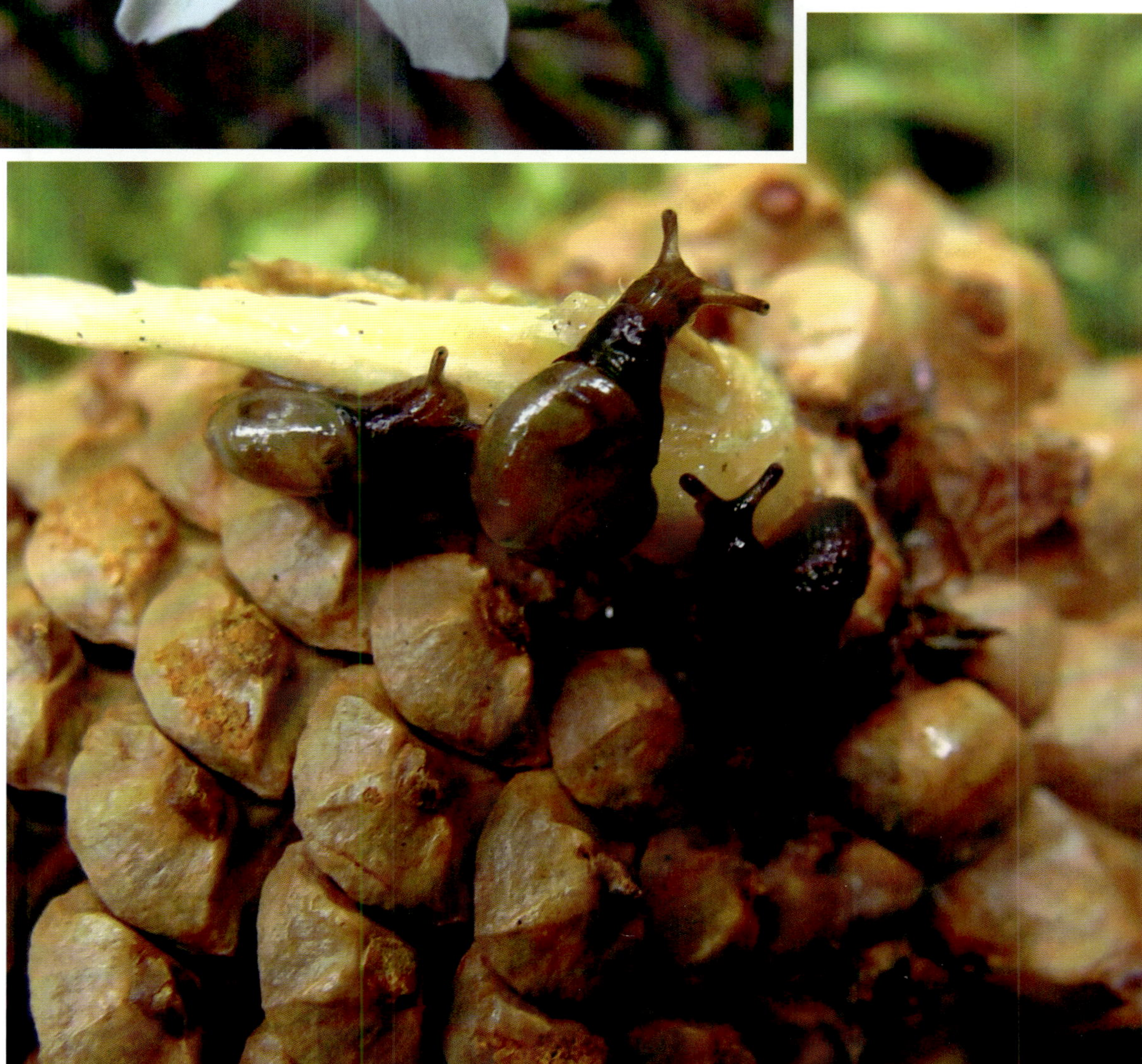

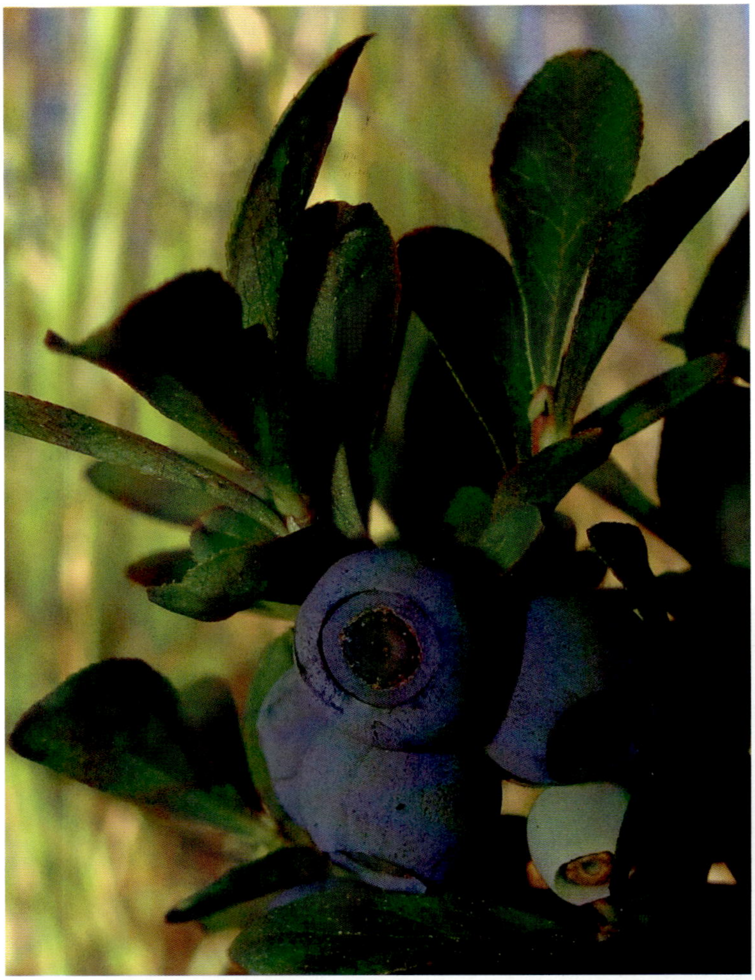

Savor
the tangy
sweetness of a
wild blueberry
or strawberry
on your tongue.

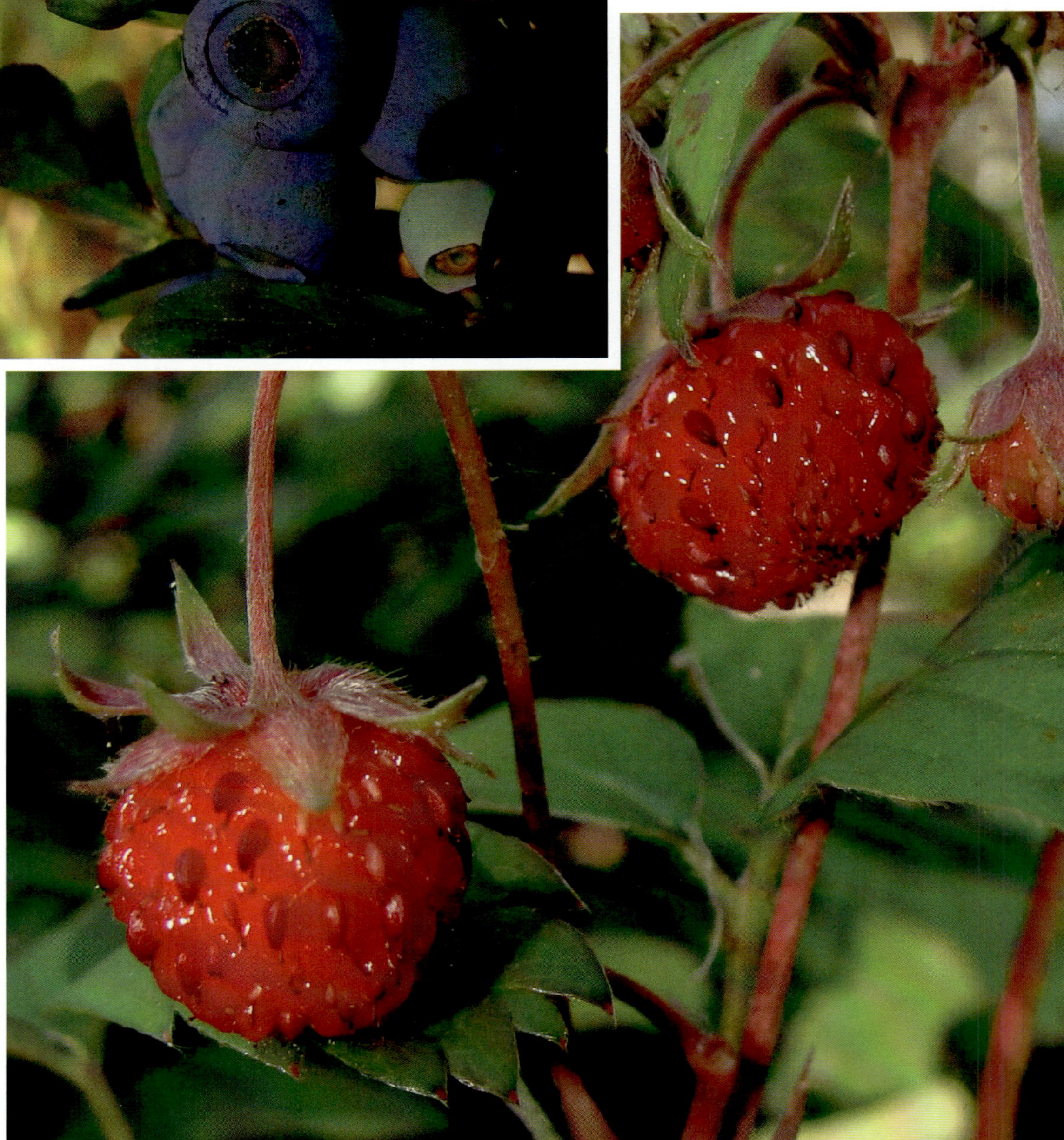

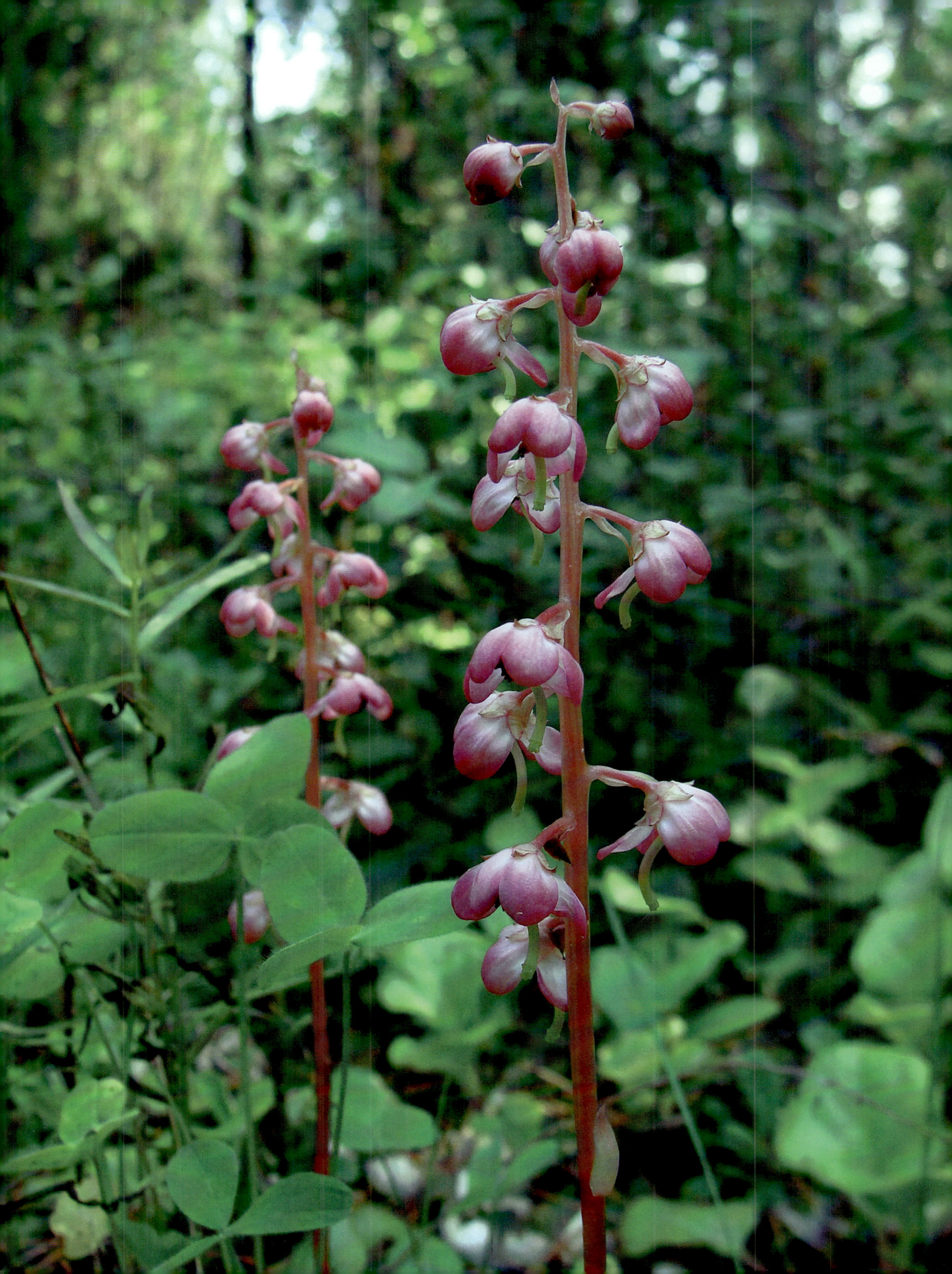

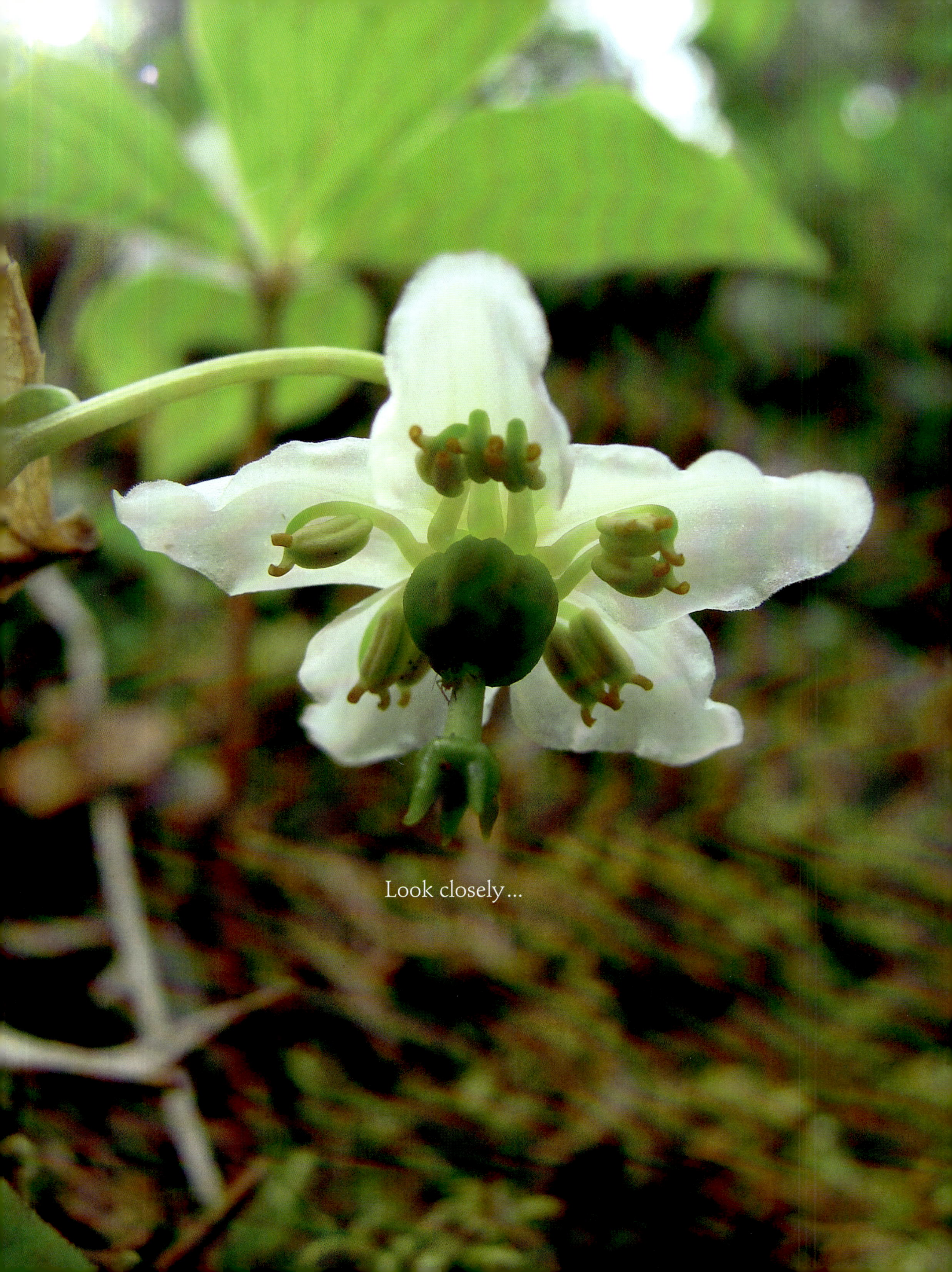
Look closely…

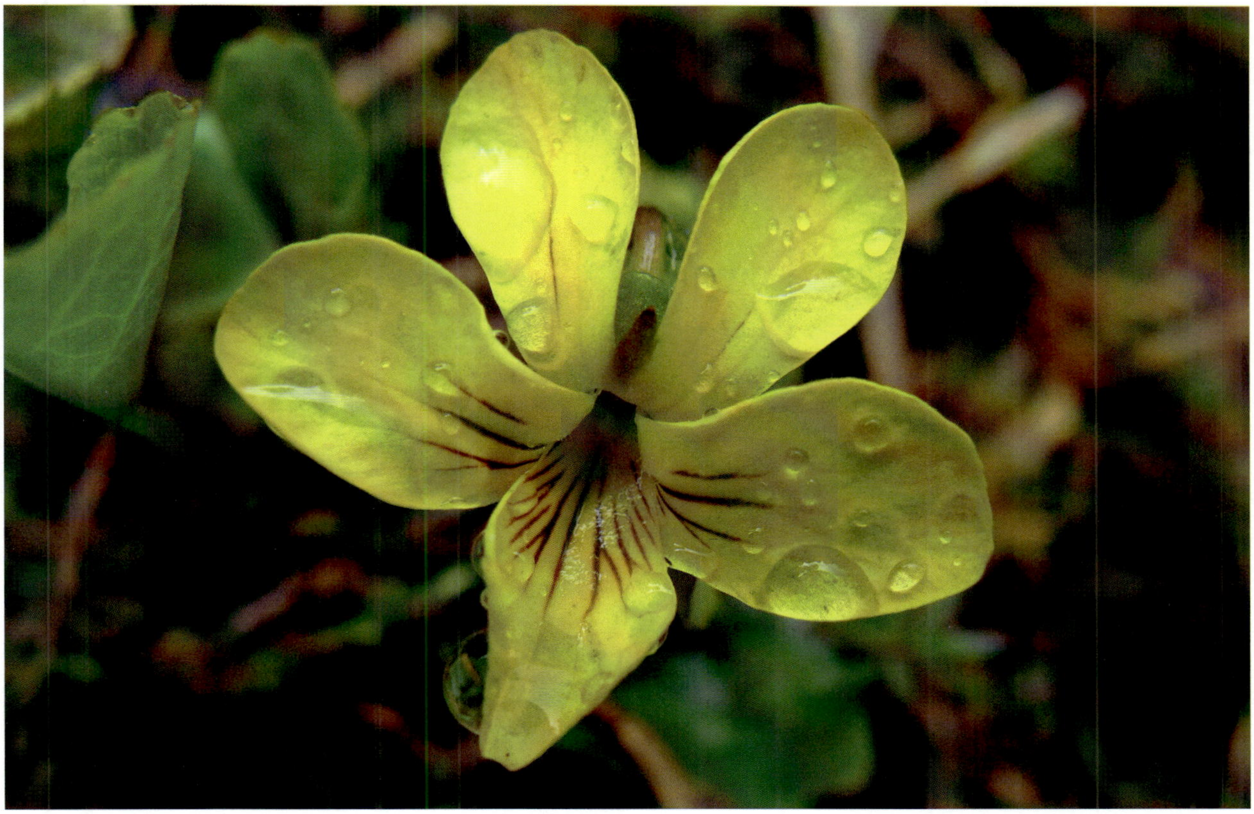

... at the flowers.

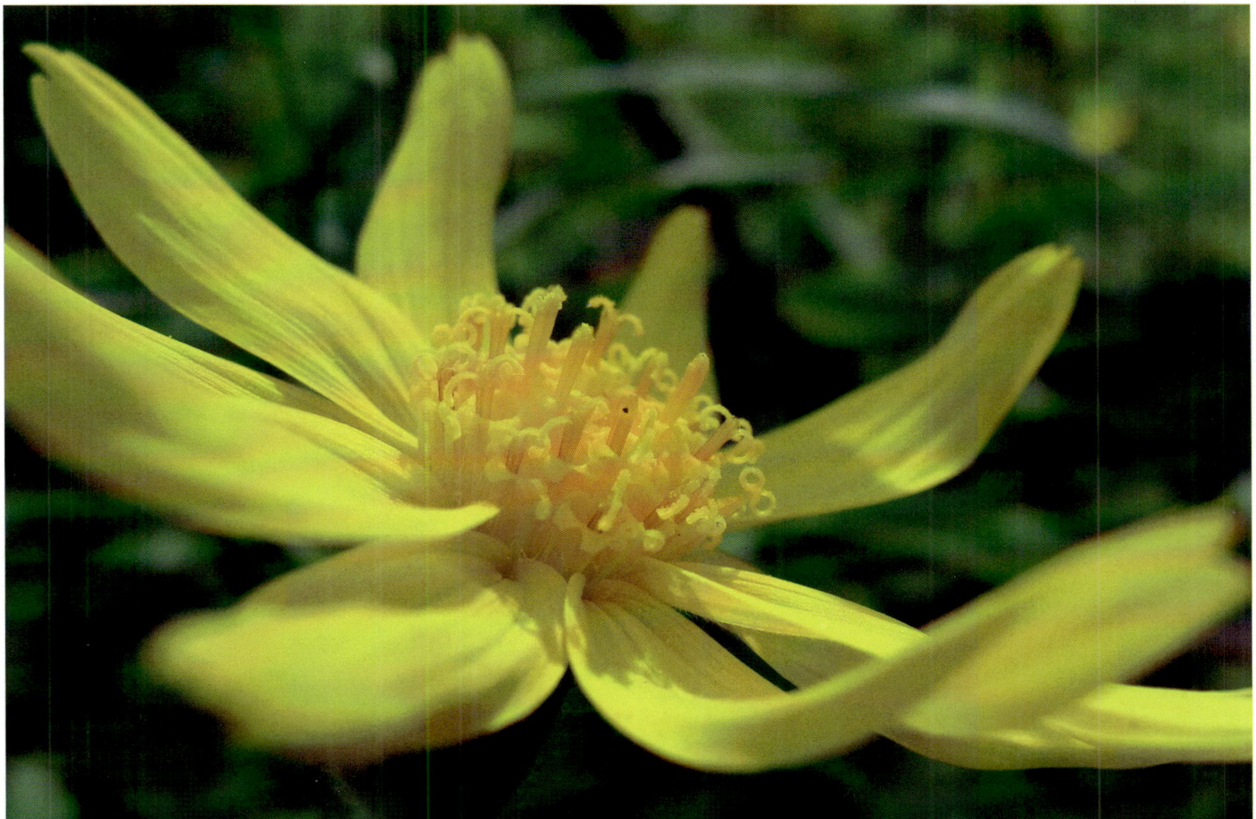

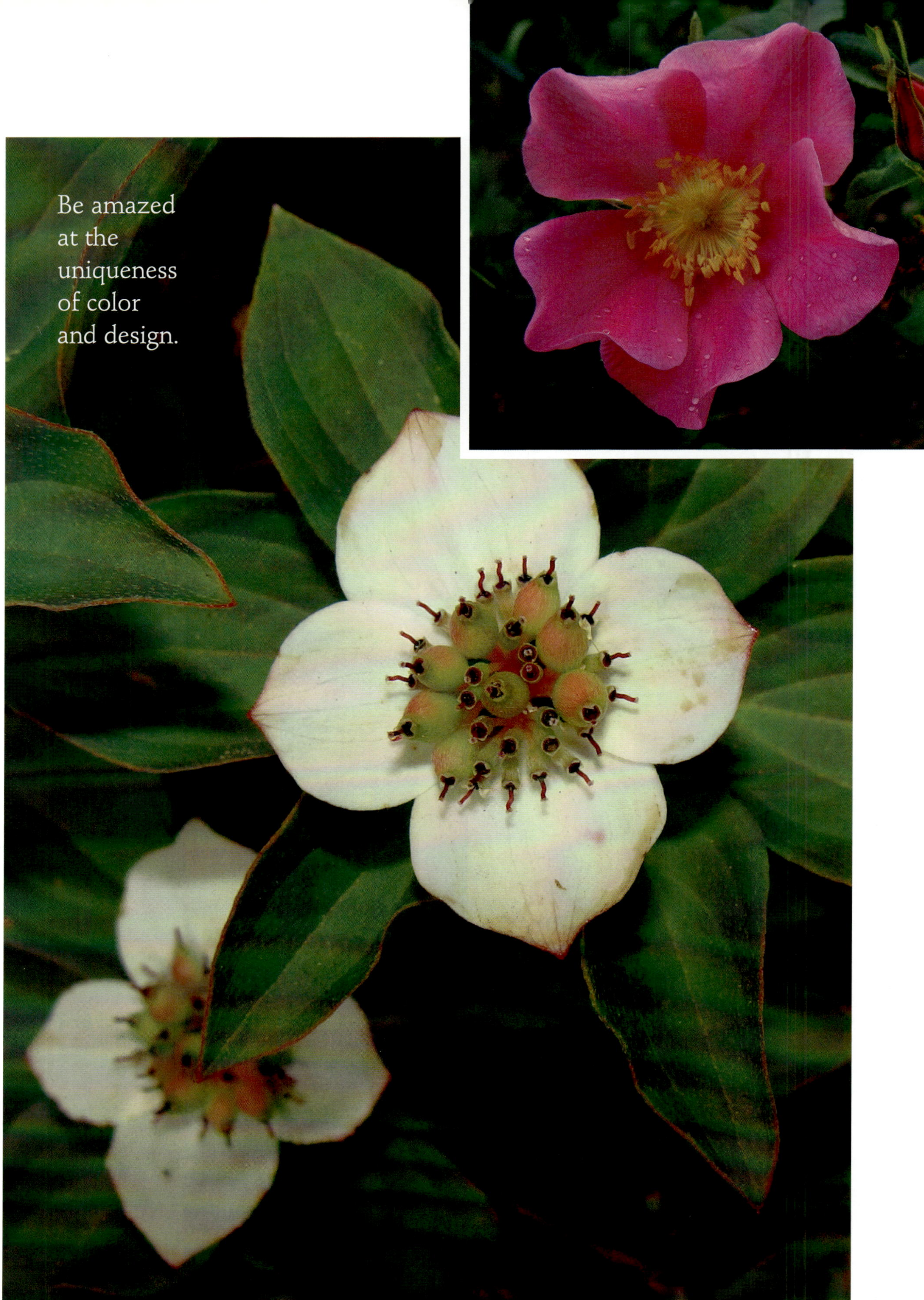

Be amazed at the uniqueness of color and design.

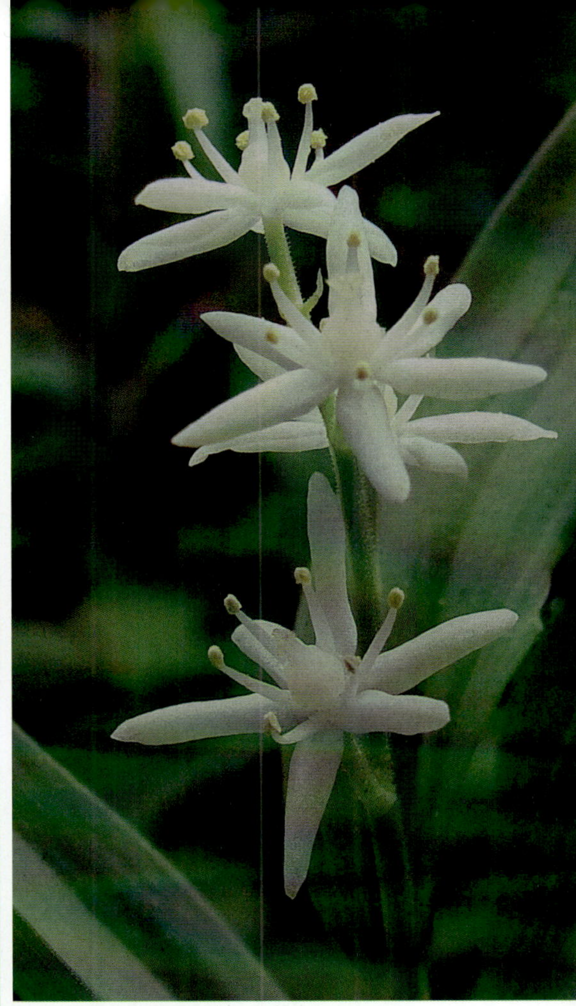

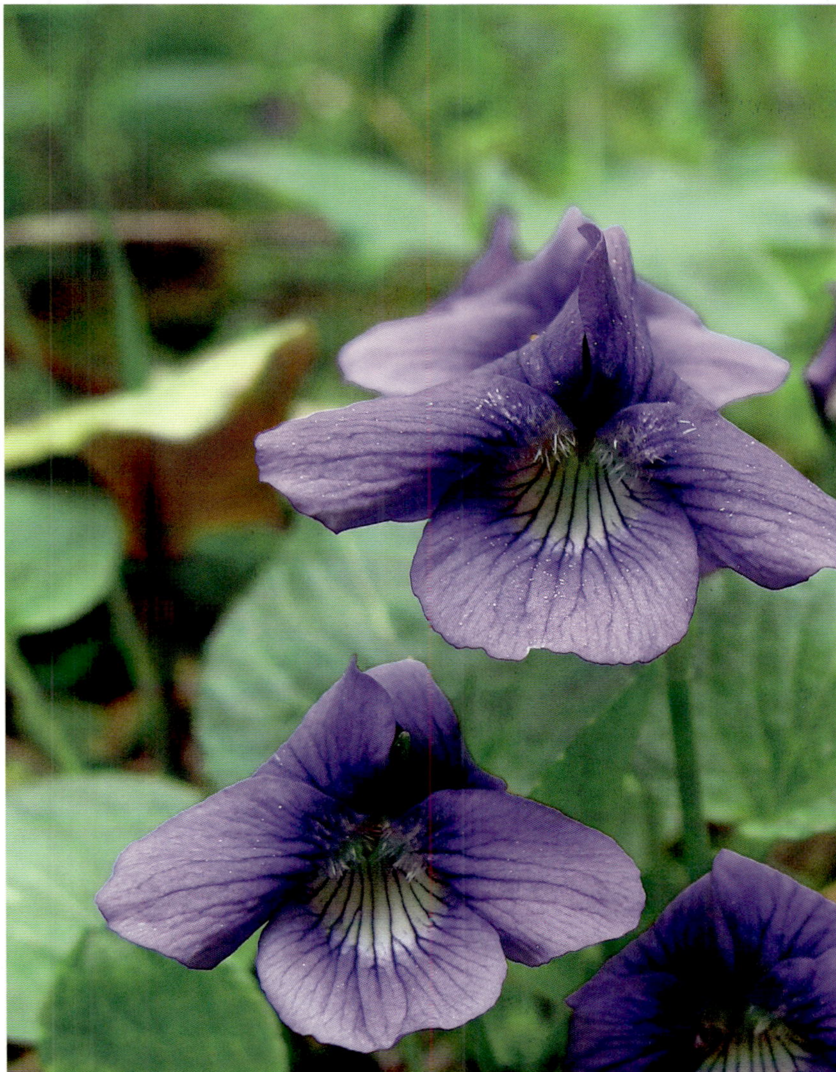

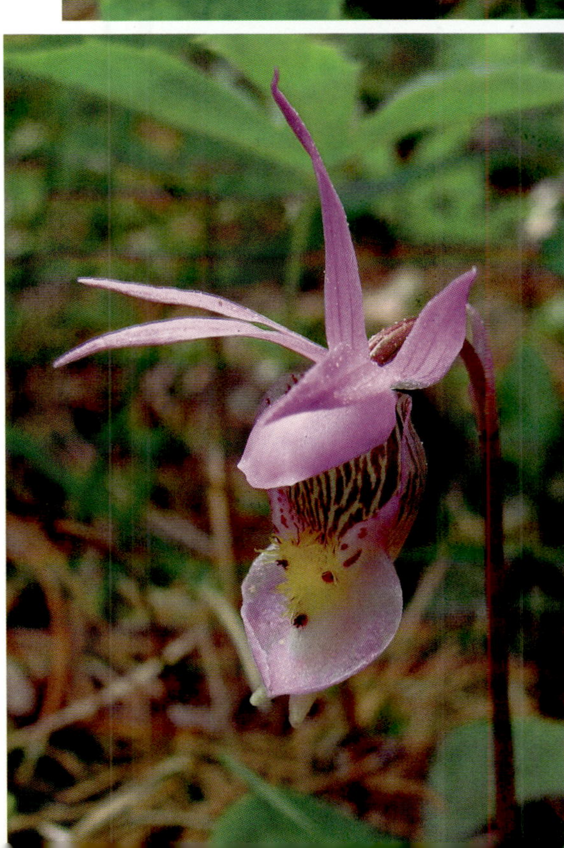

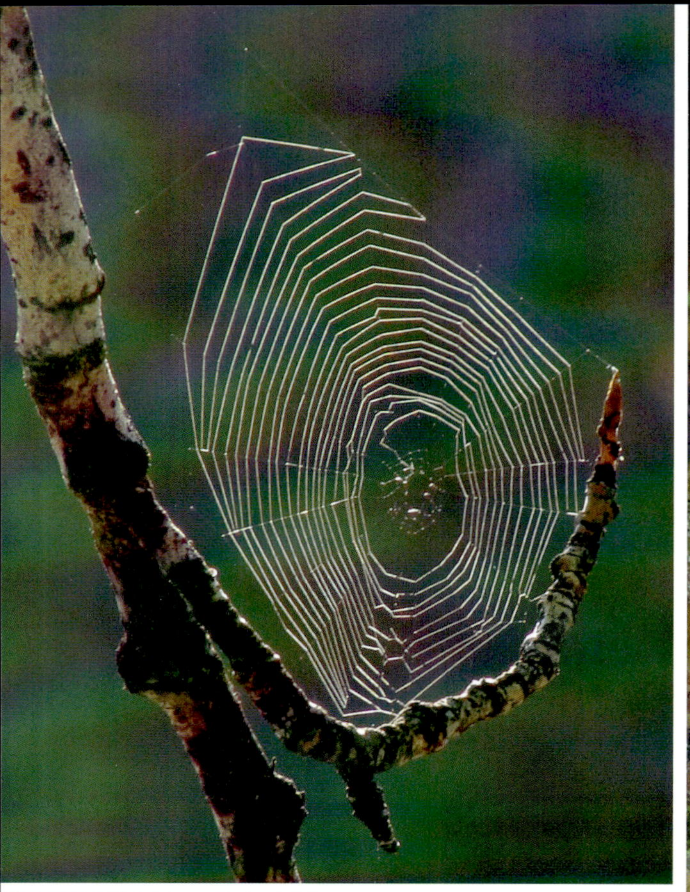

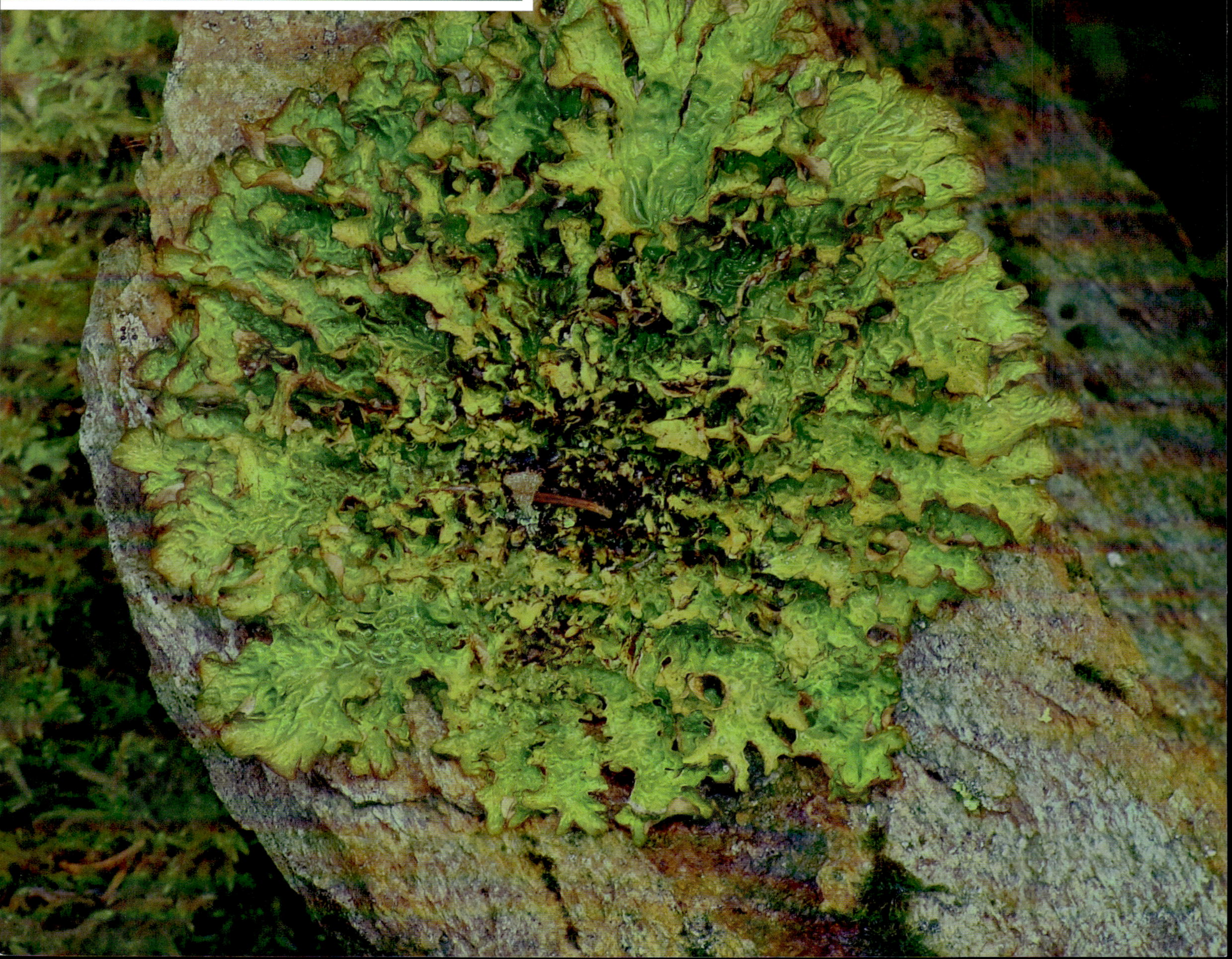

Spider webs,
mosses,
and lichens ...

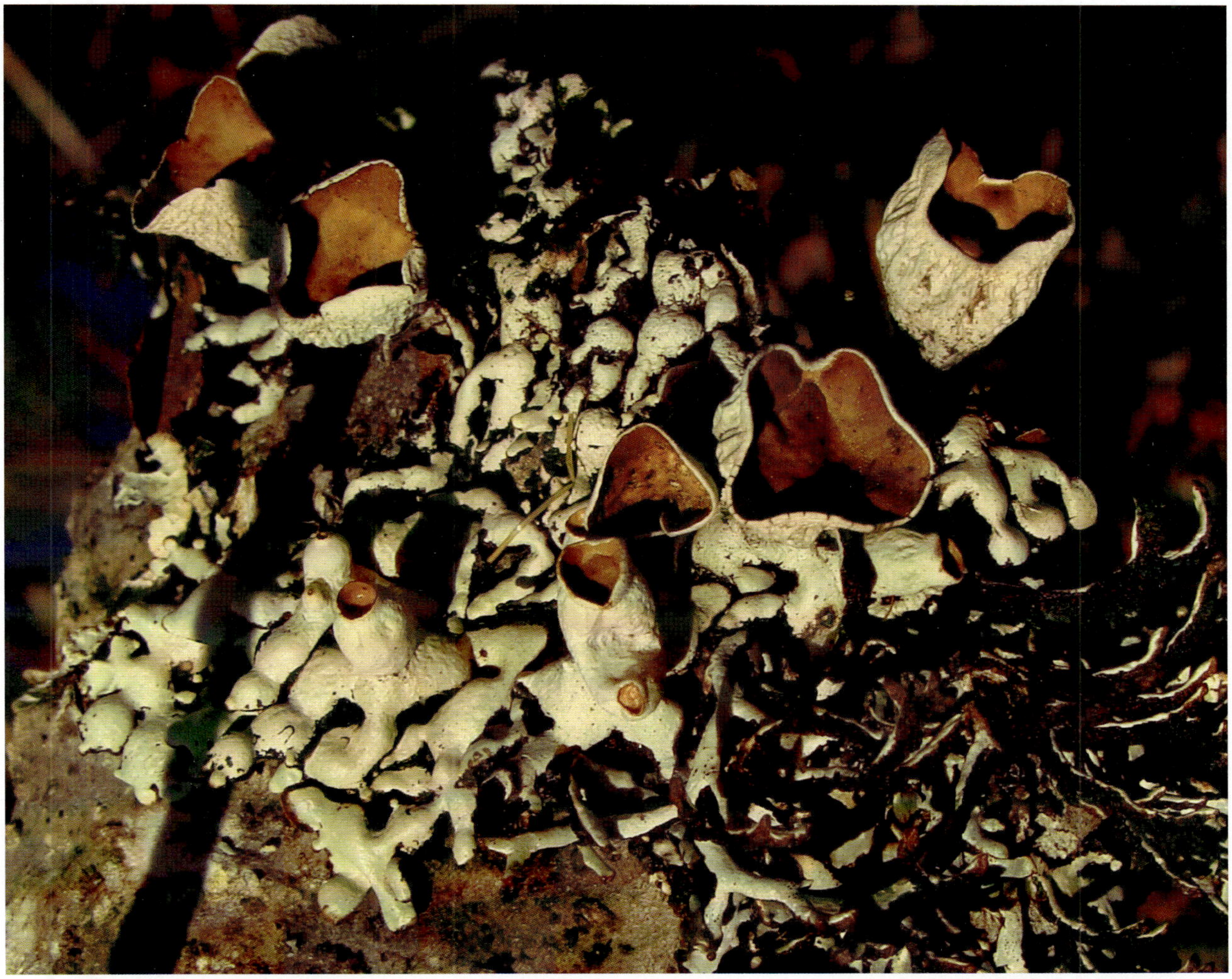

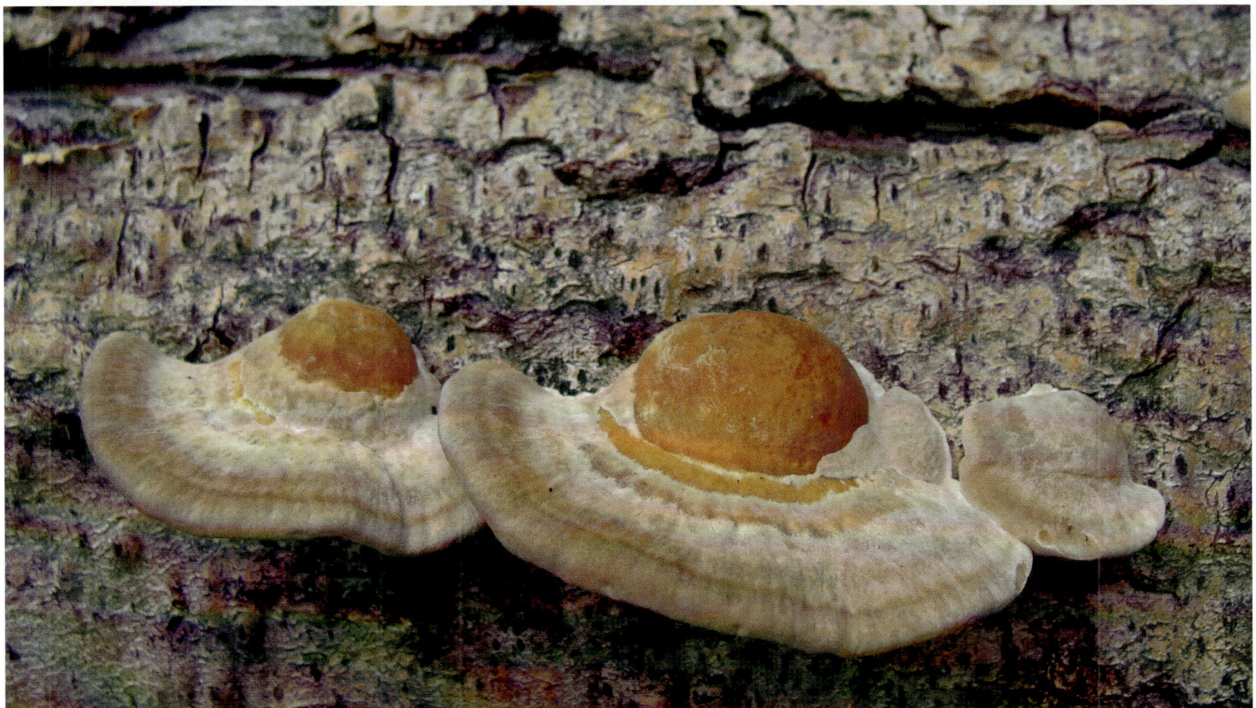

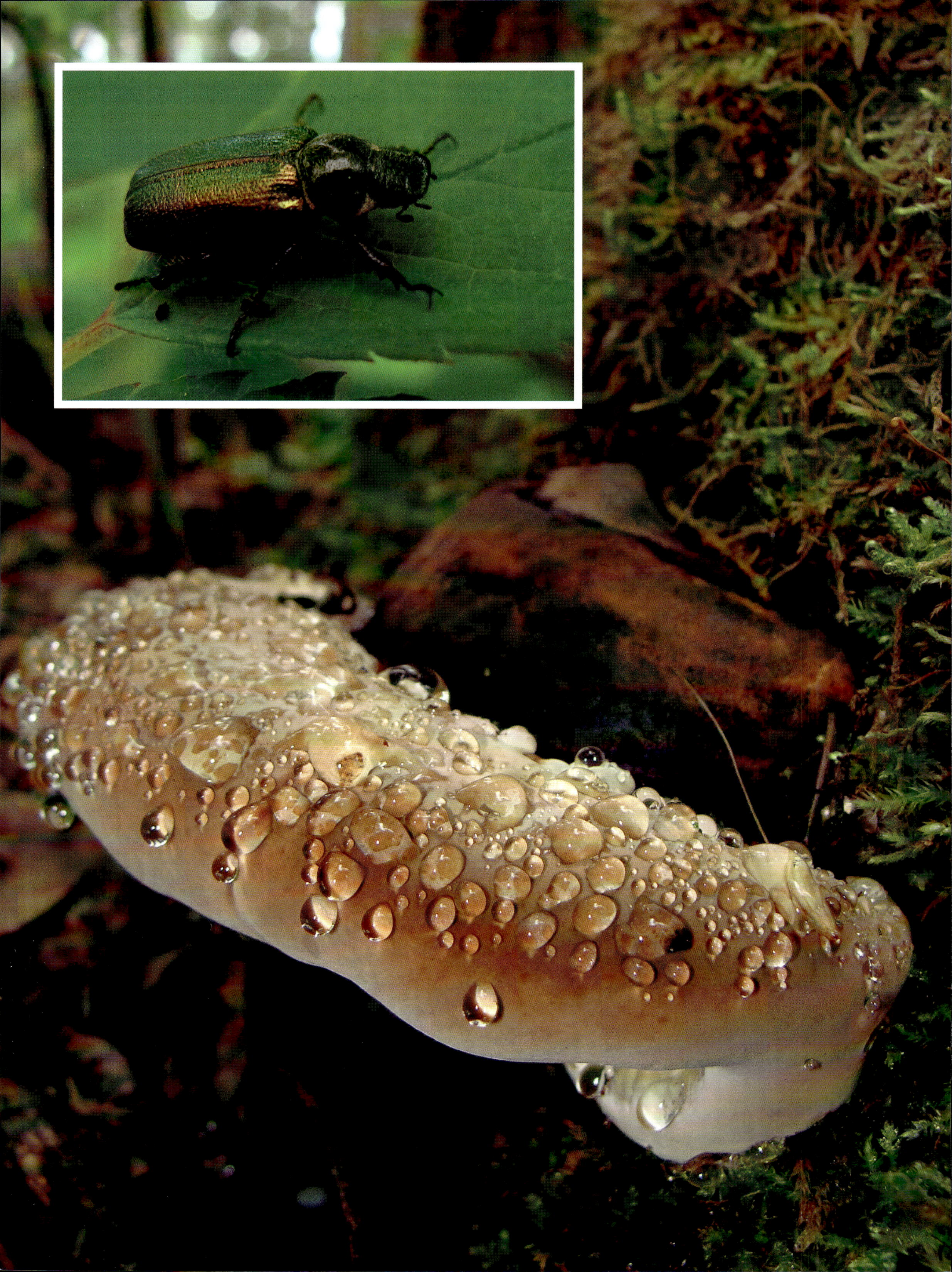

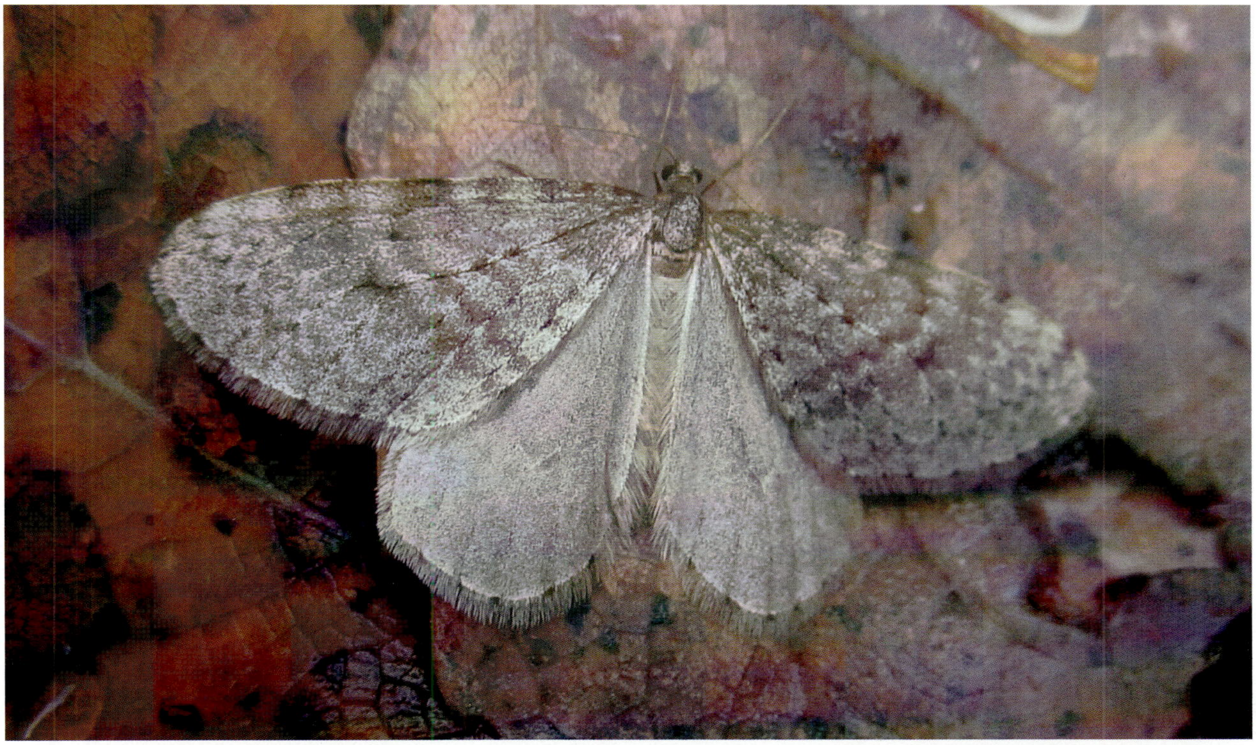

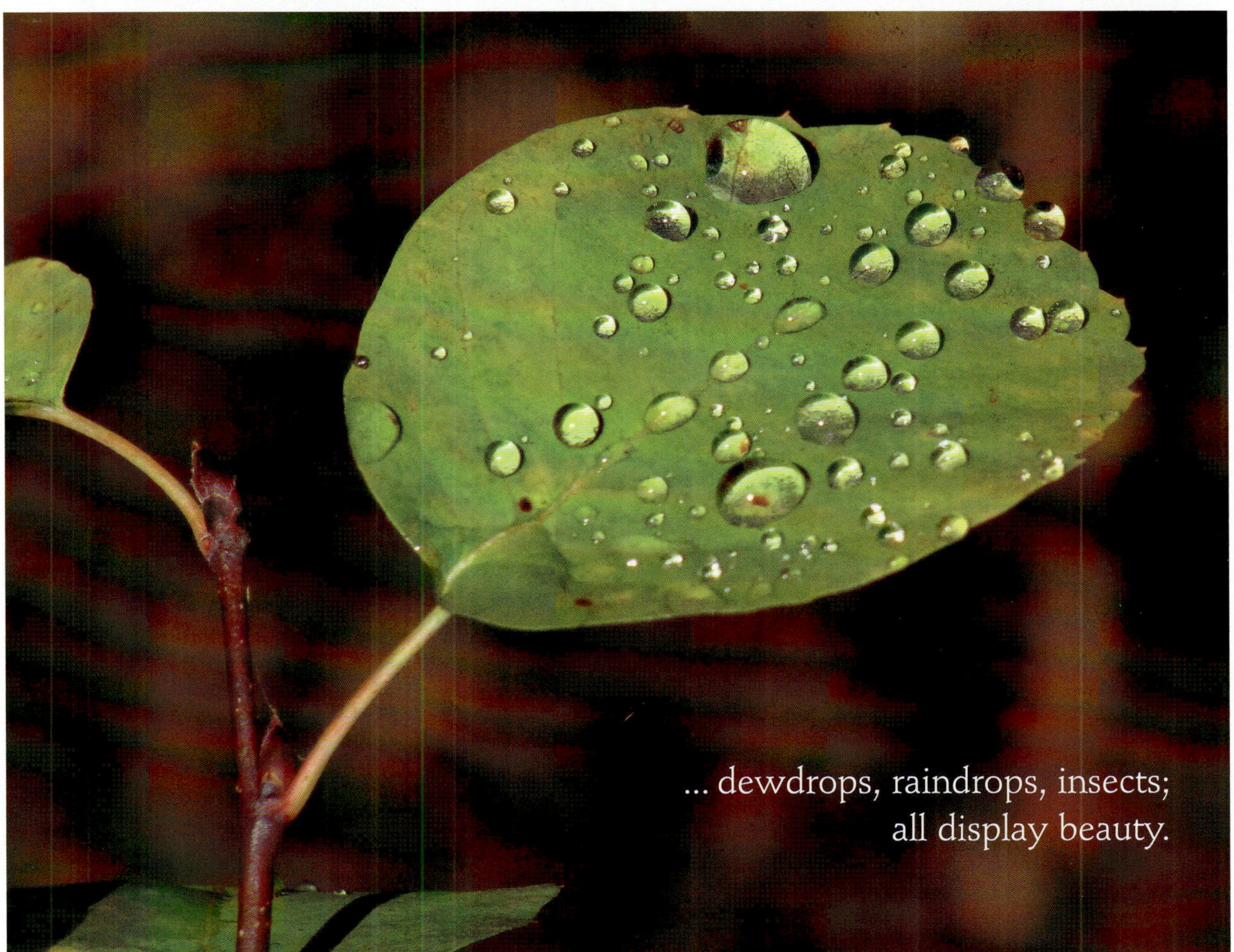

... dewdrops, raindrops, insects;
all display beauty.

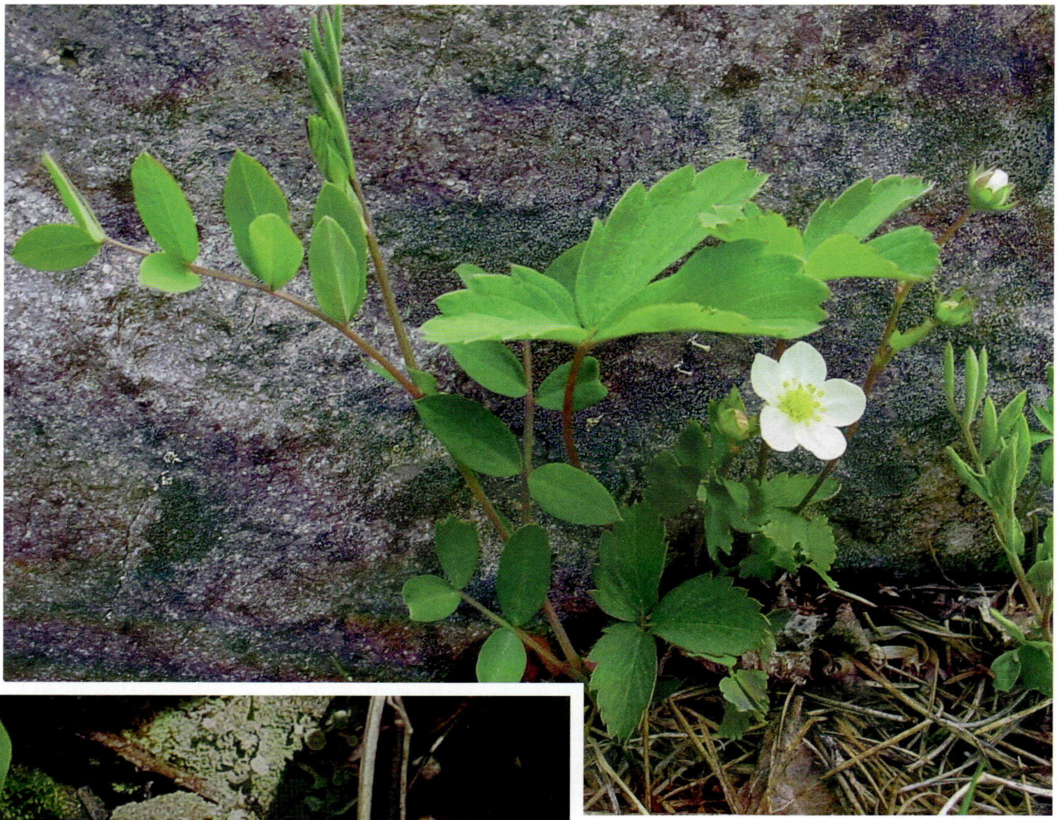

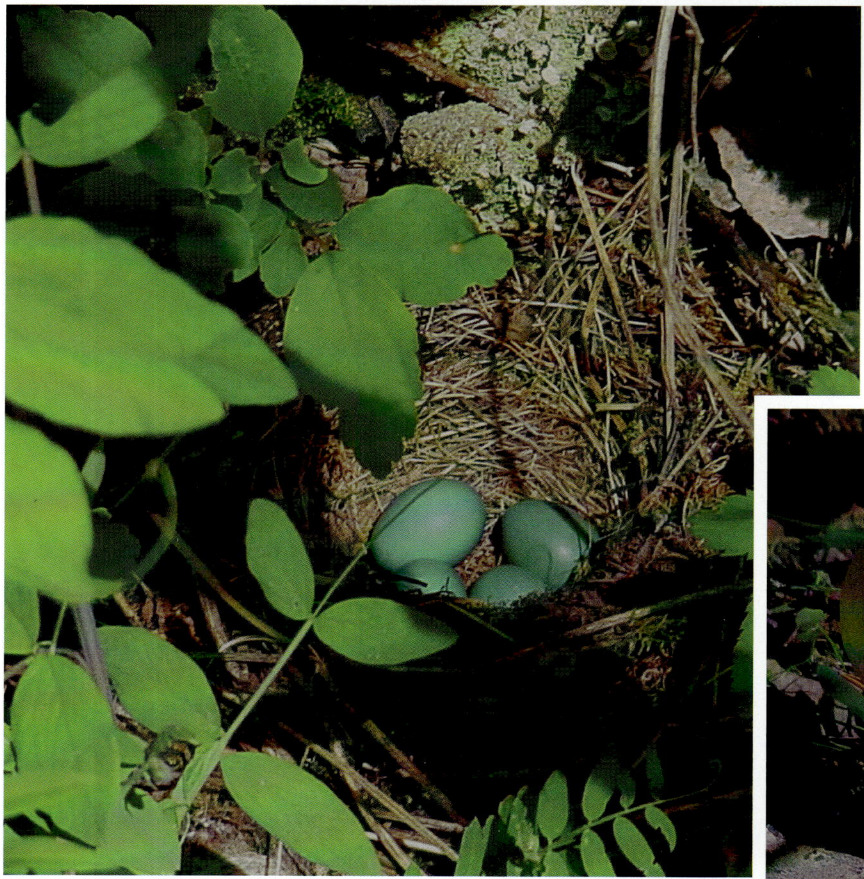

Seeing these
small bits
of God's
handiwork ...

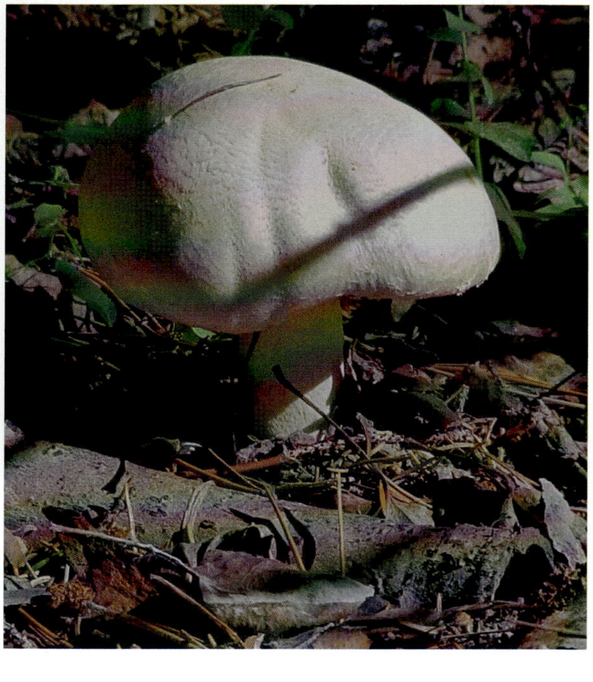

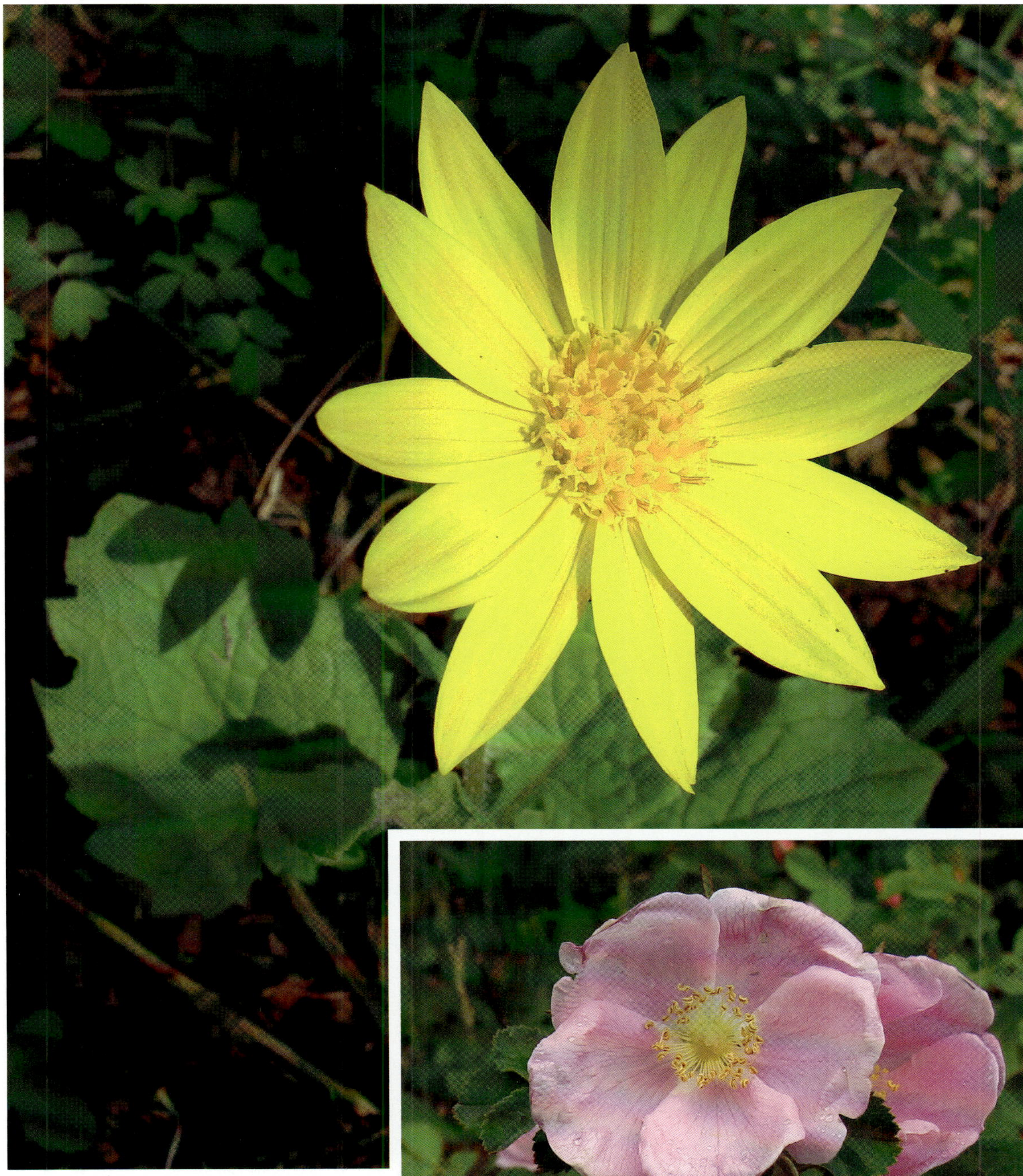

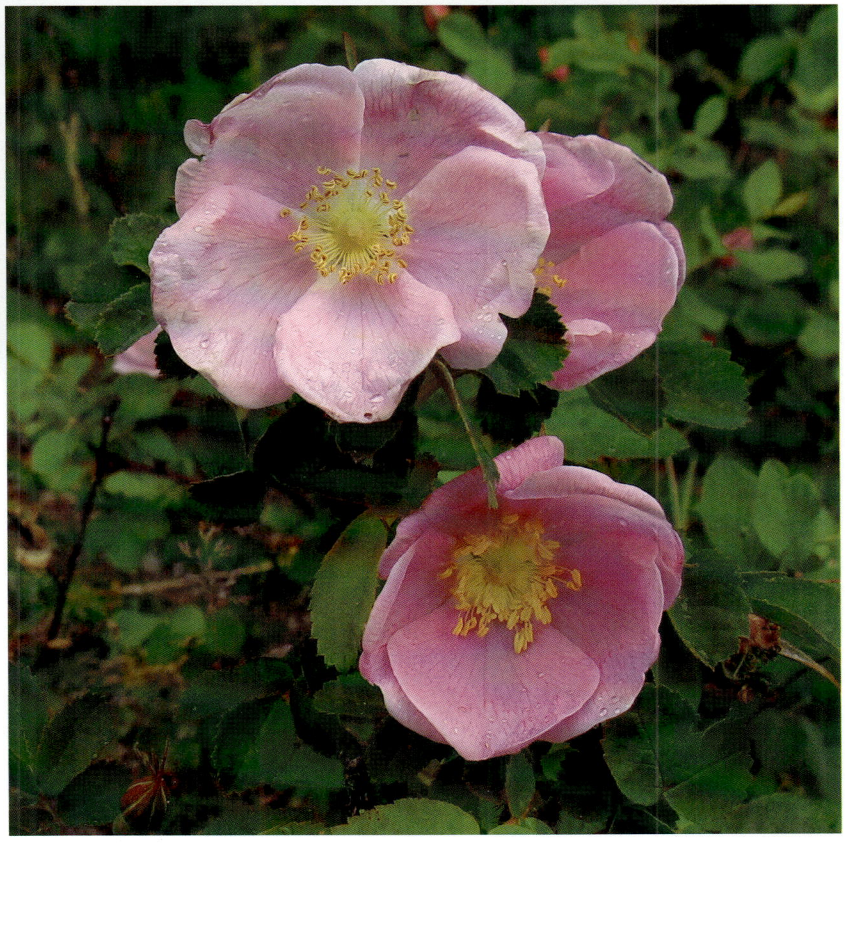

... brings delight
and eases
tension.

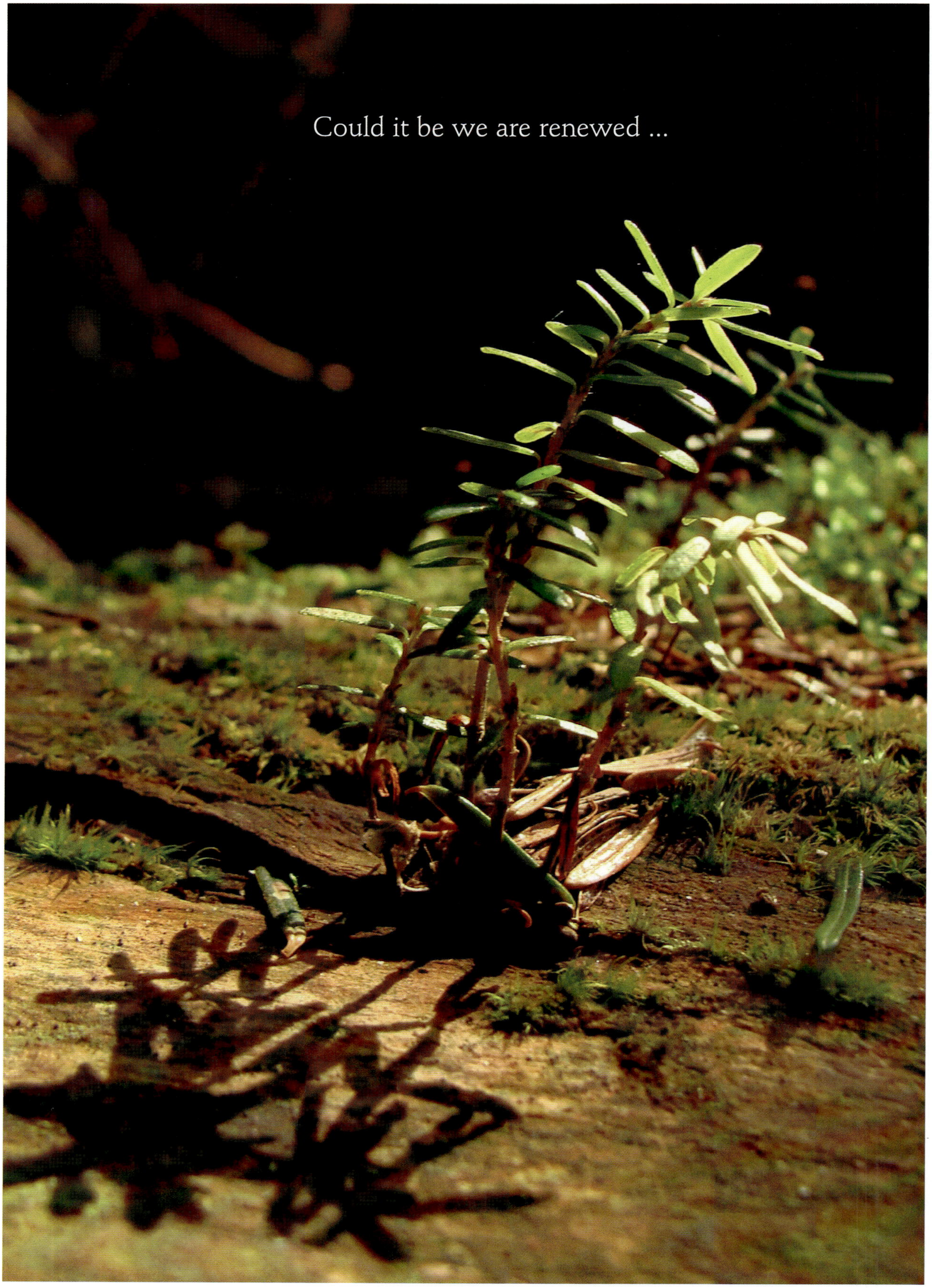
Could it be we are renewed ...

... because His presence is there?

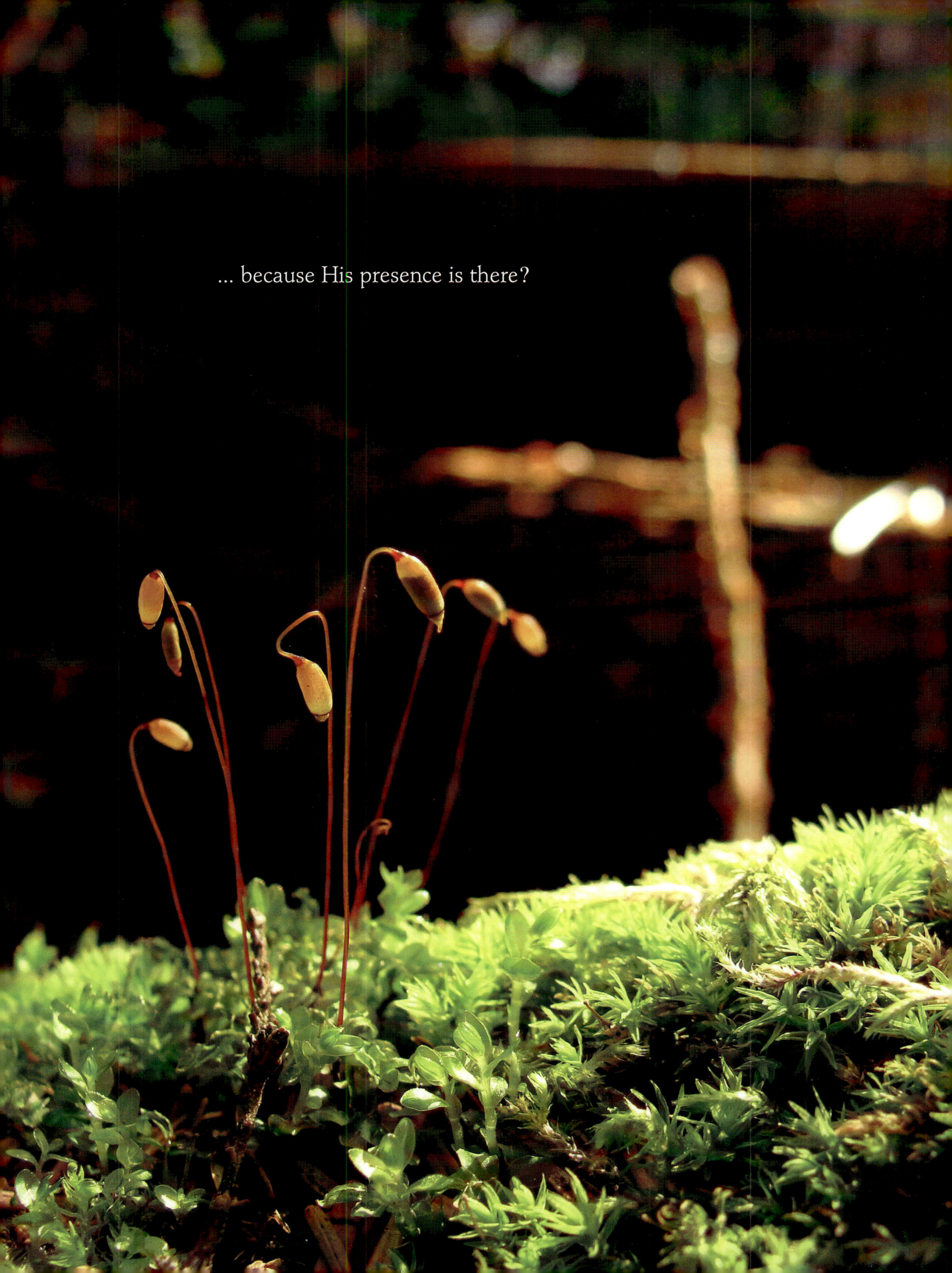

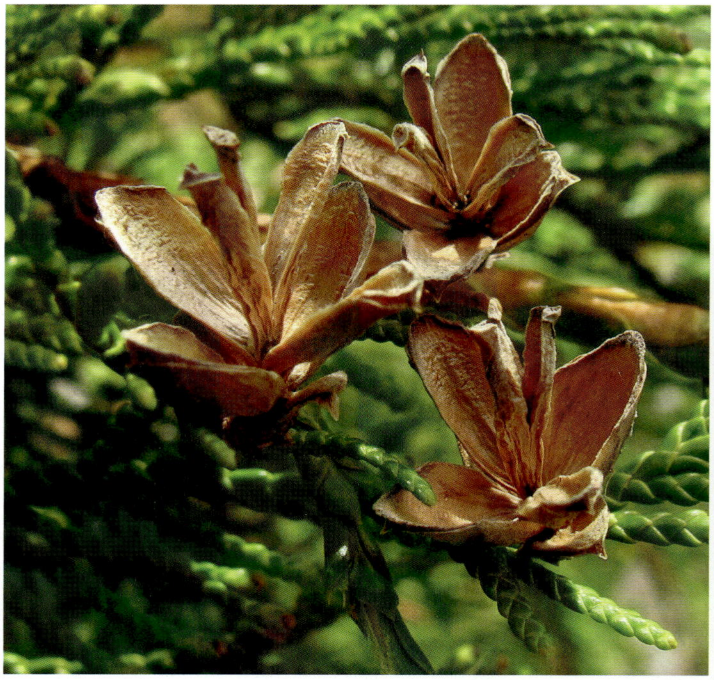

Do we see the
Master Designer?

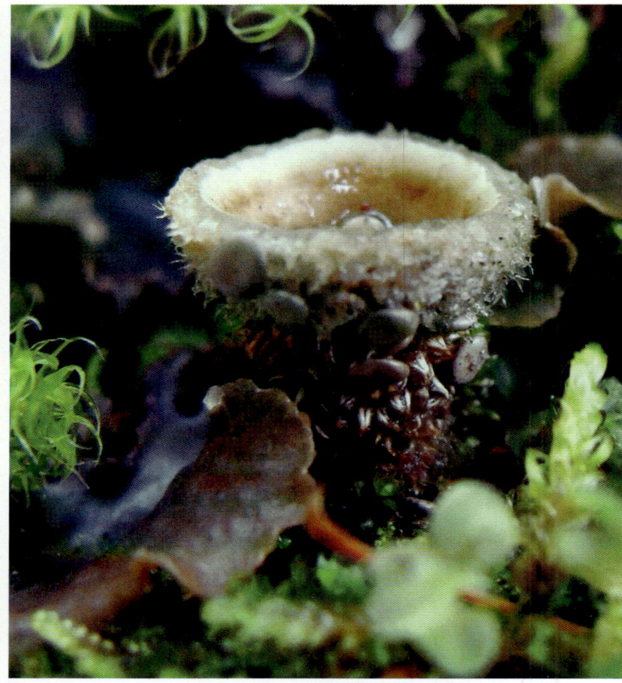

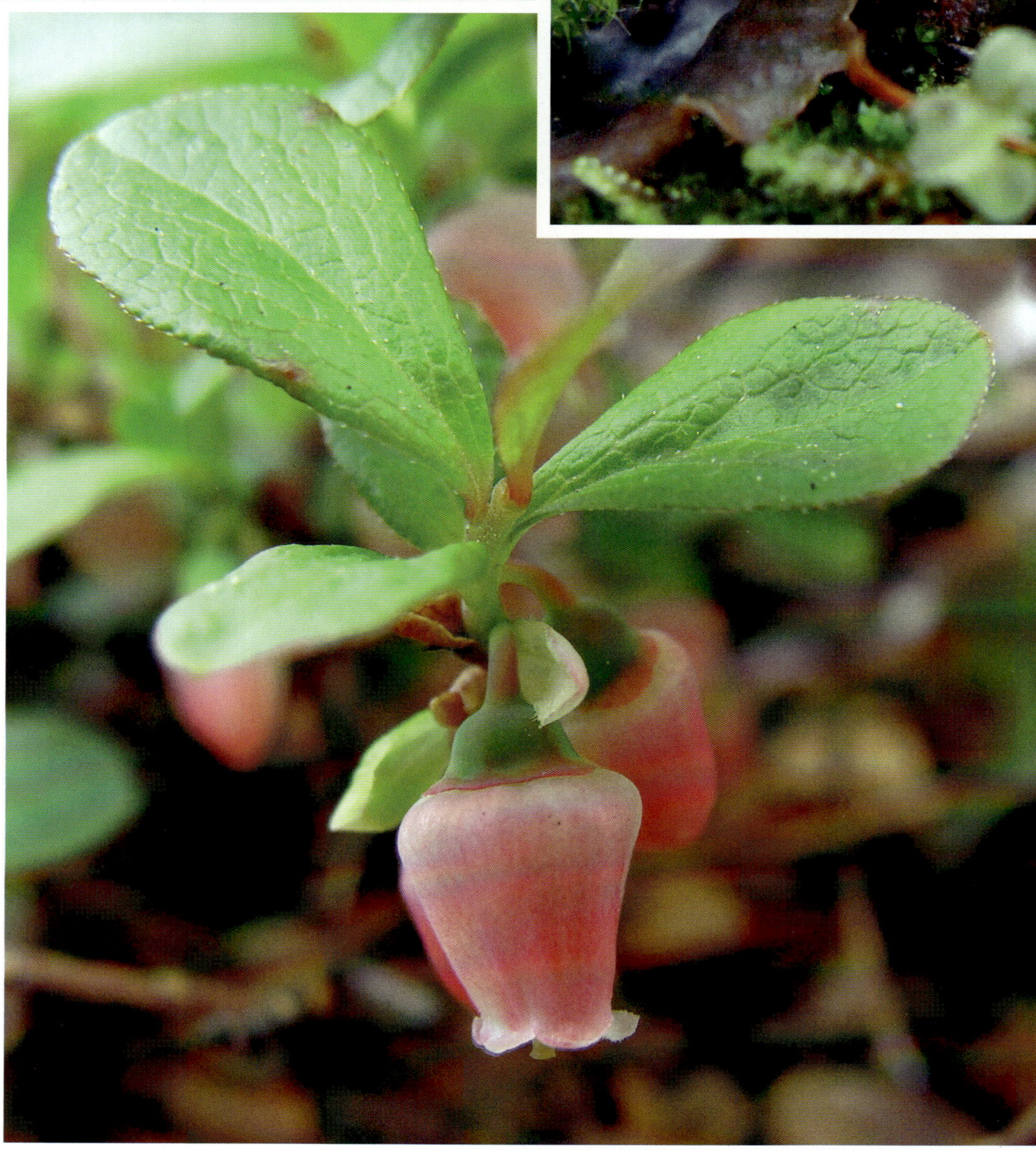

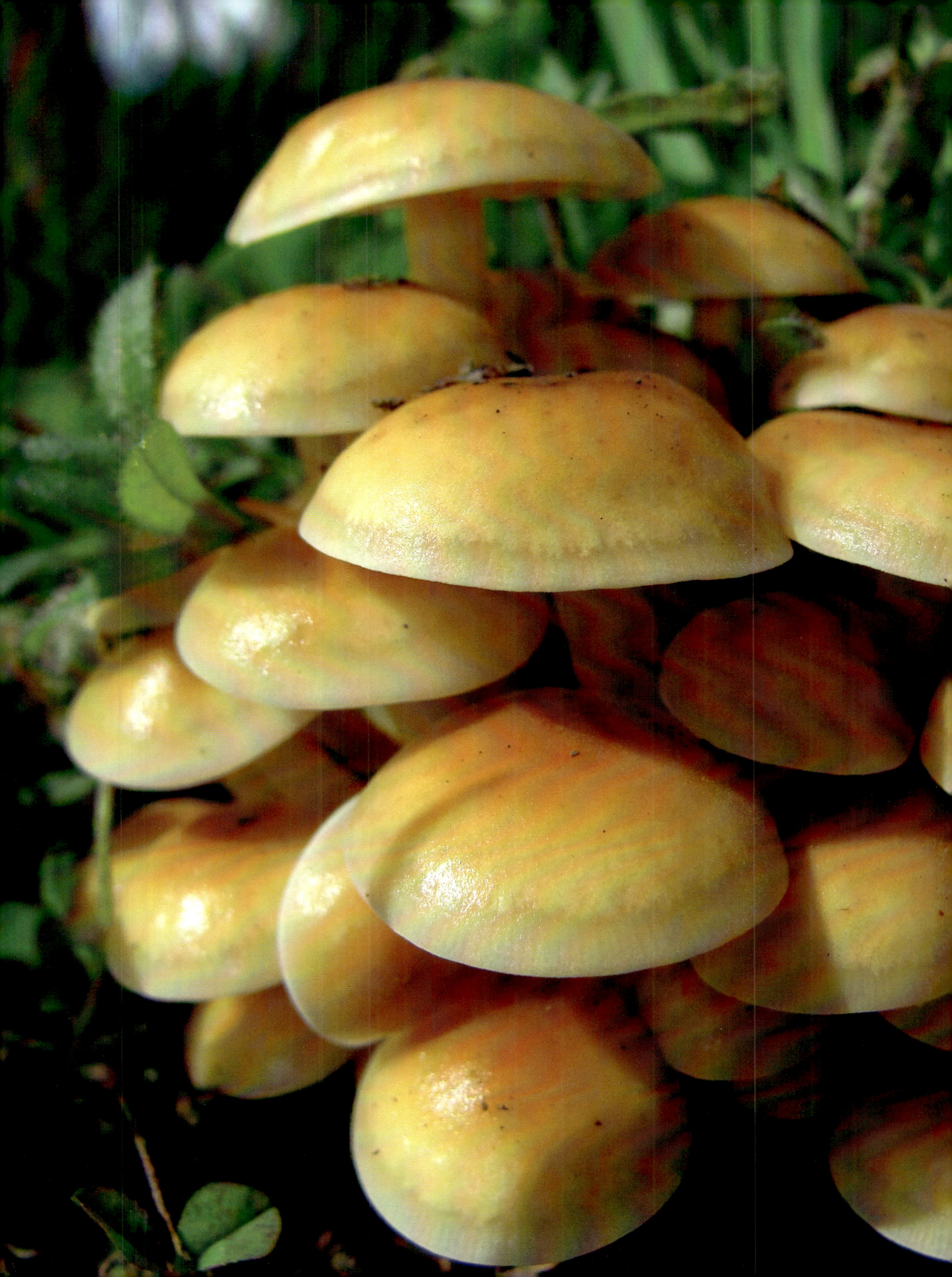

Do we experience
the pleasure of
these gifts to us?

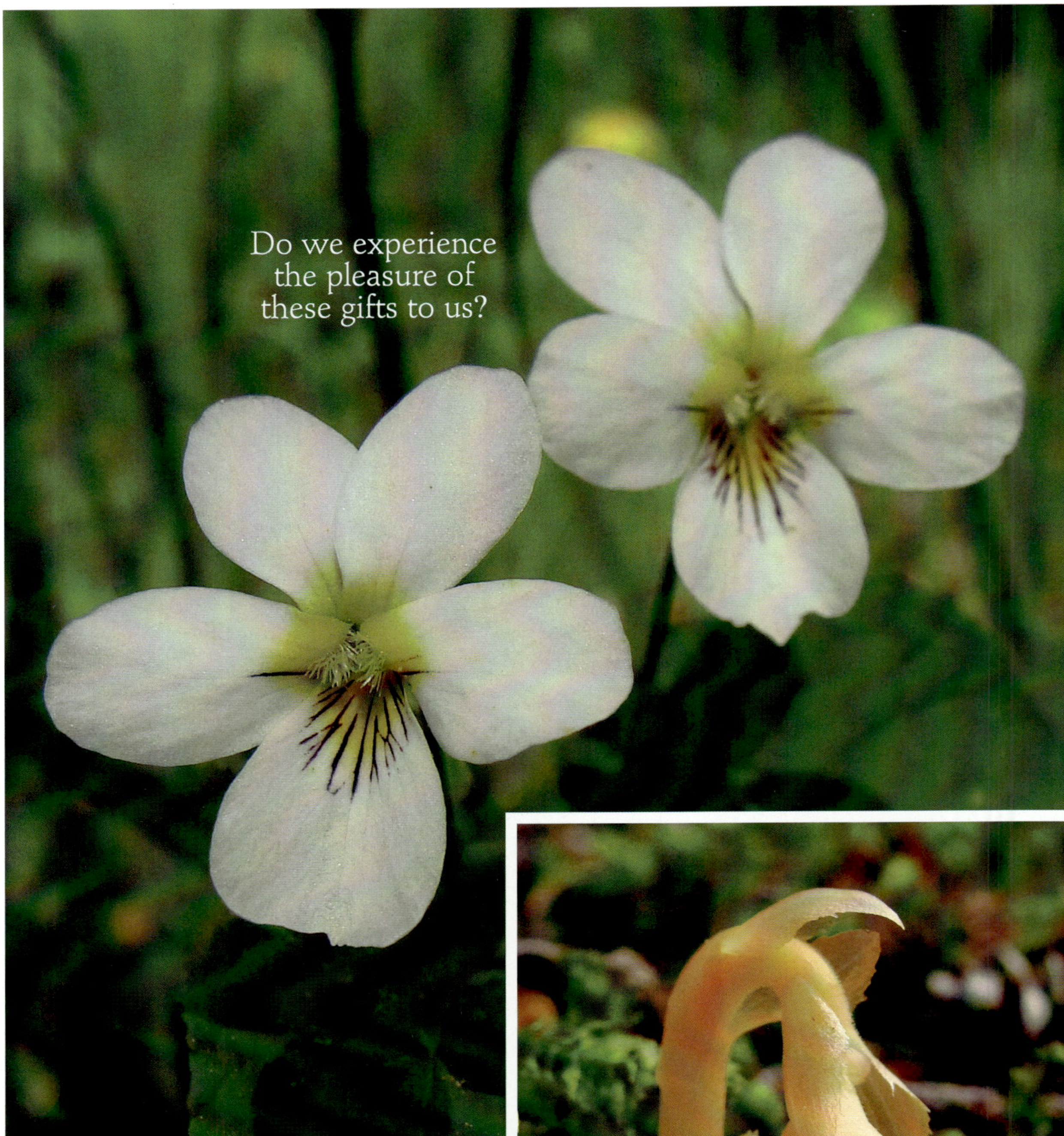

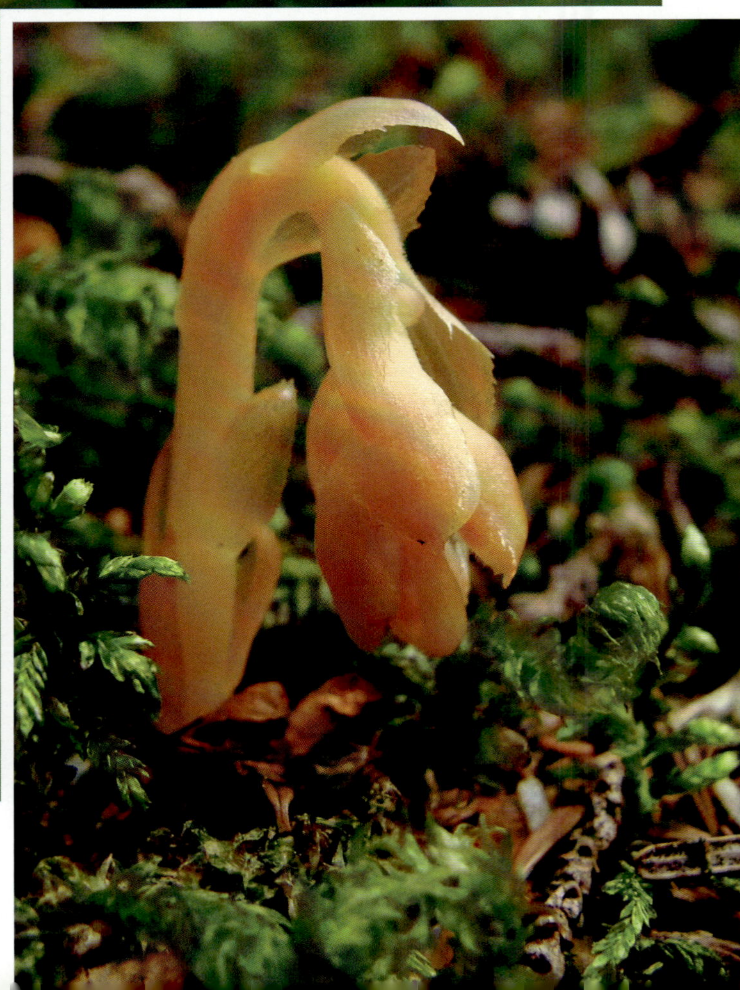

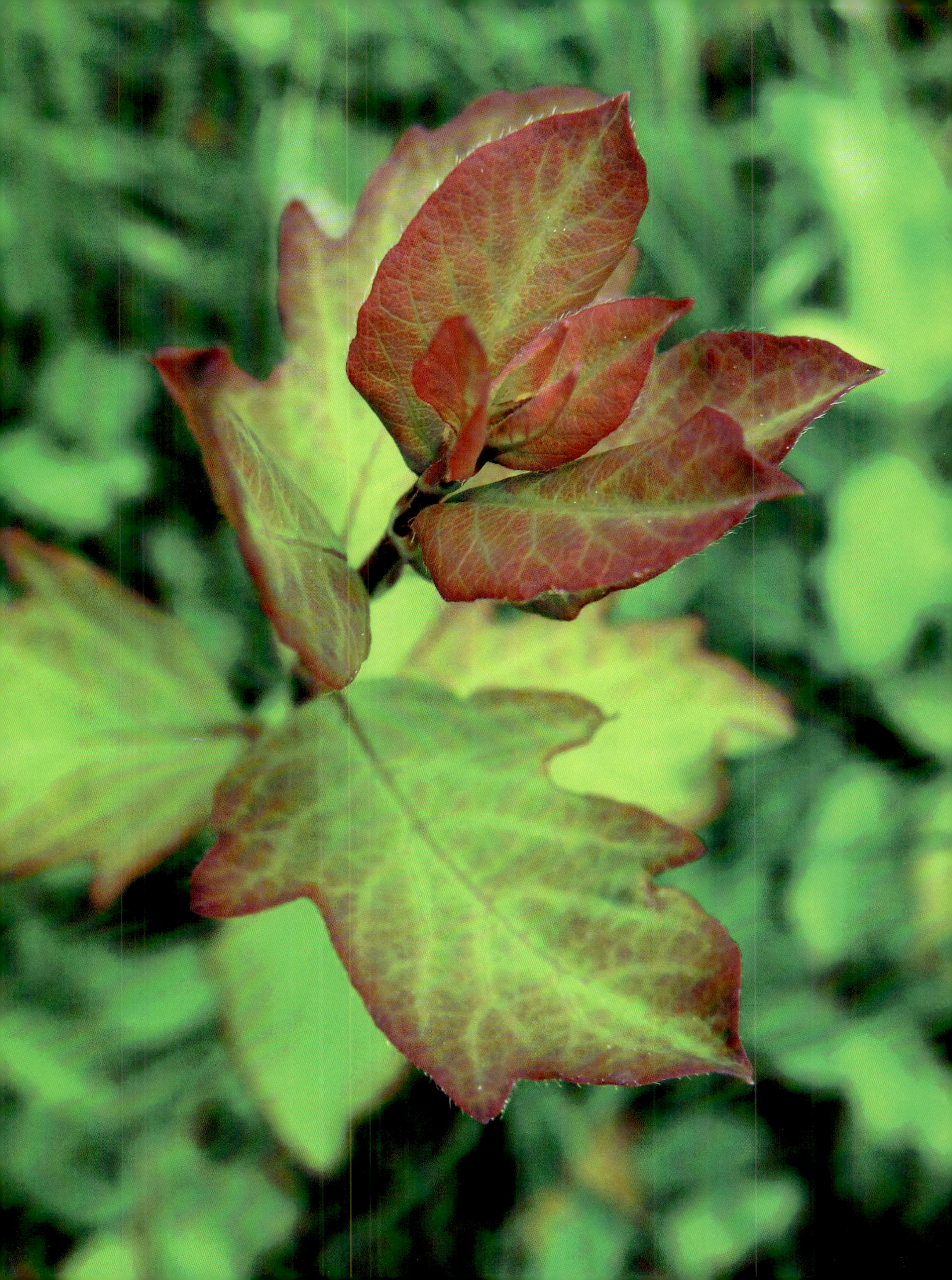

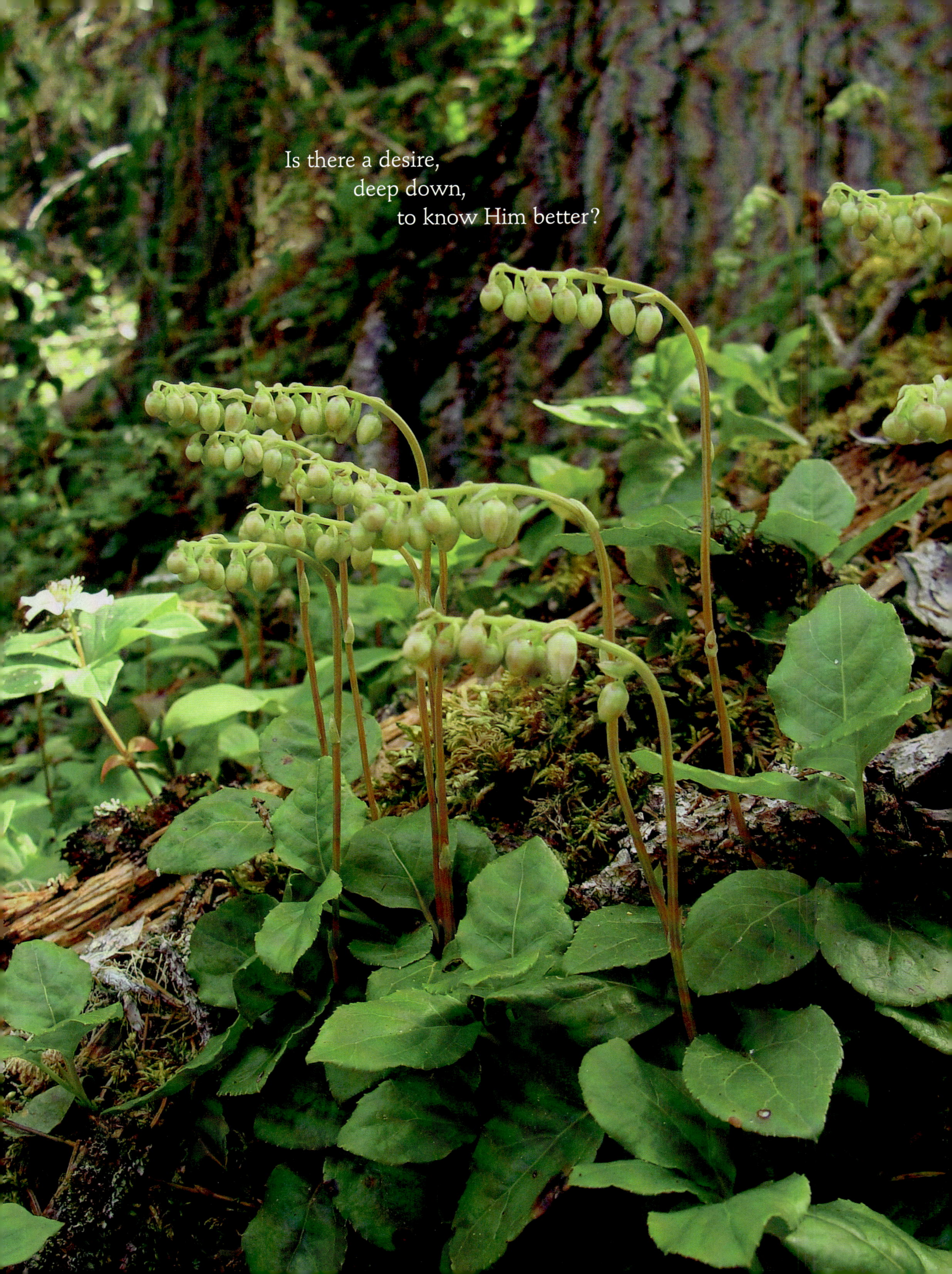
Is there a desire,
deep down,
to know Him better?

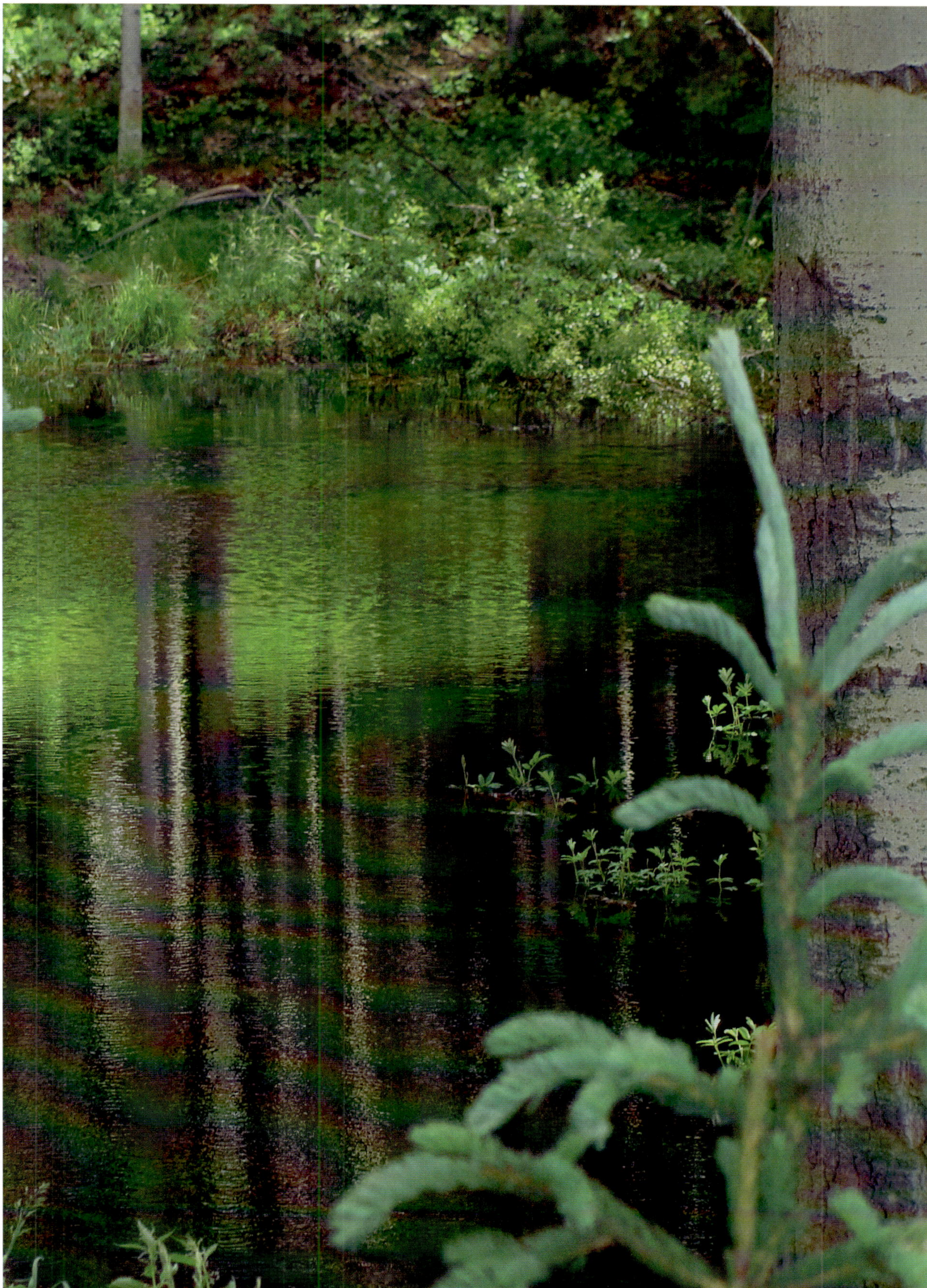

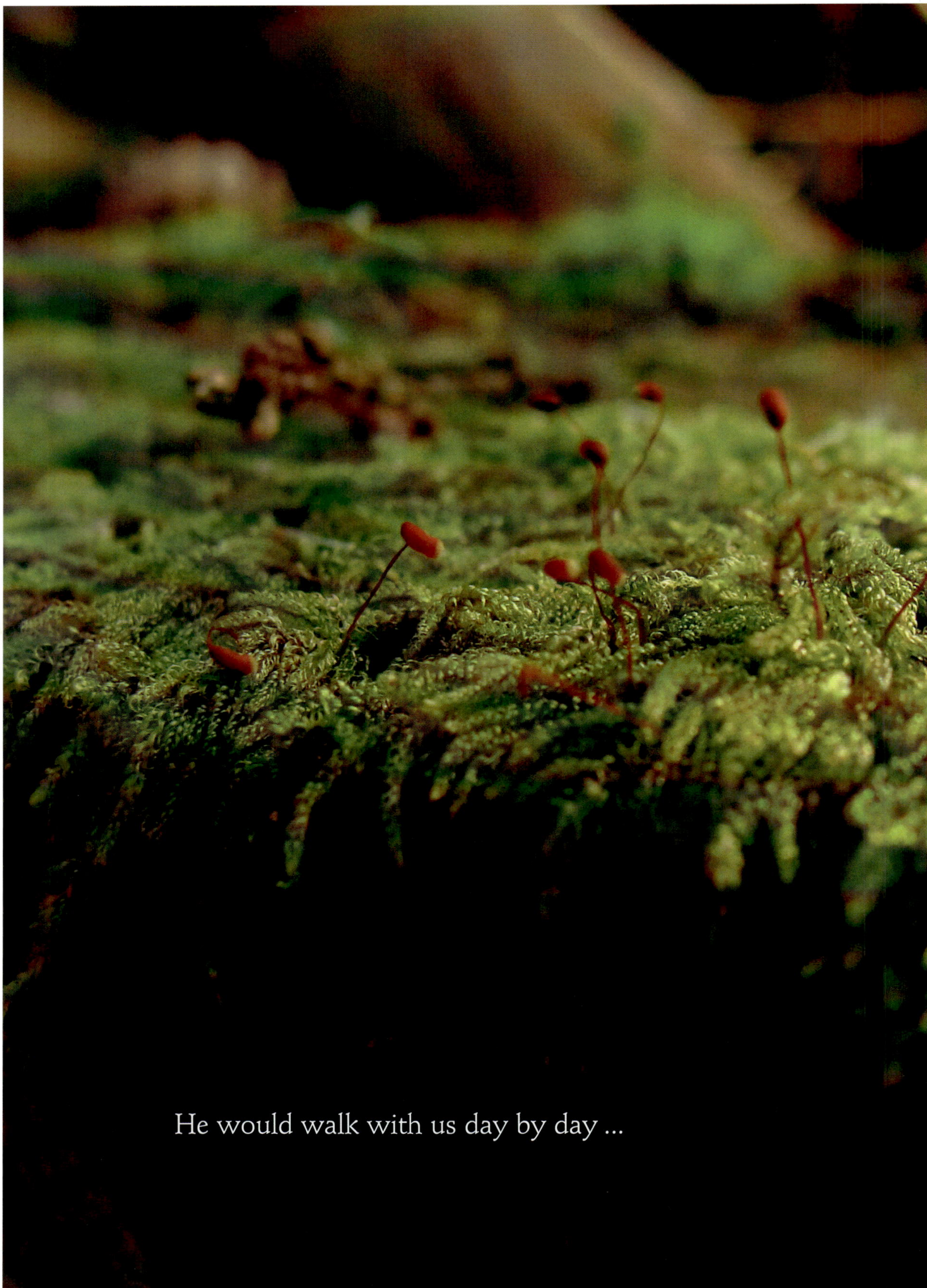
He would walk with us day by day ...

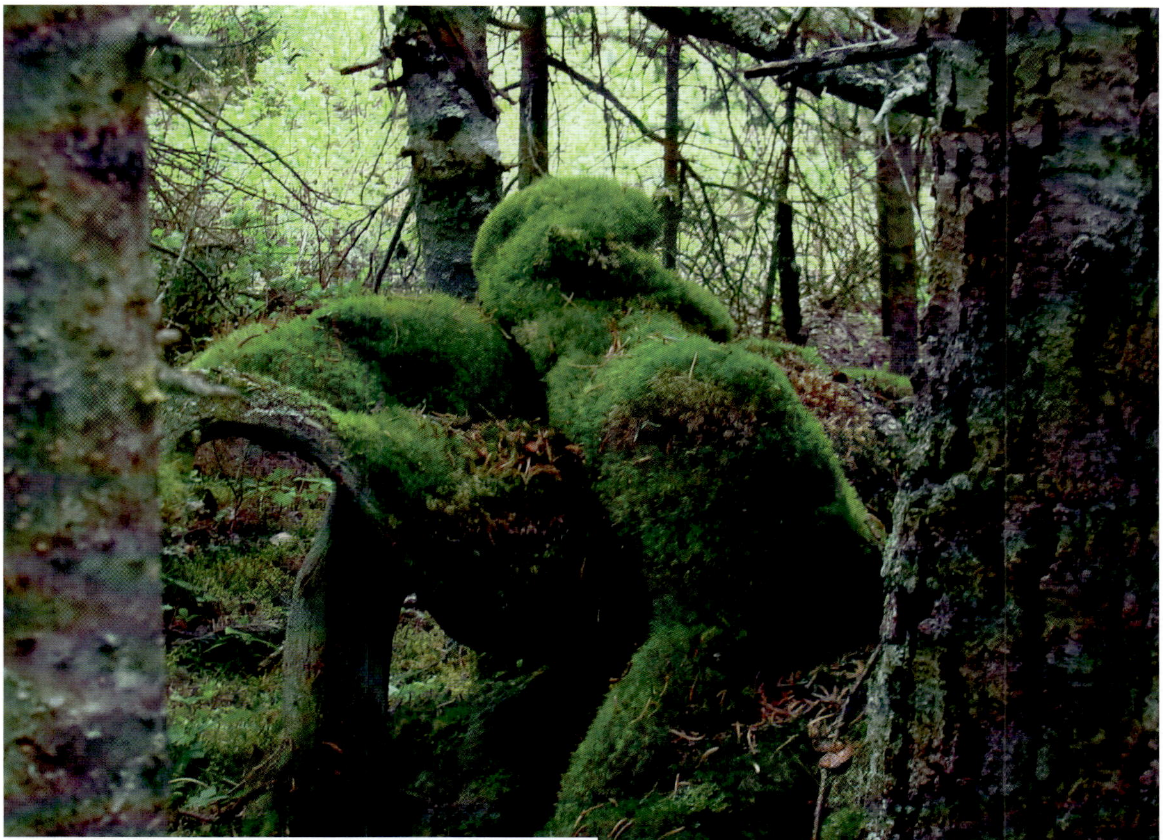

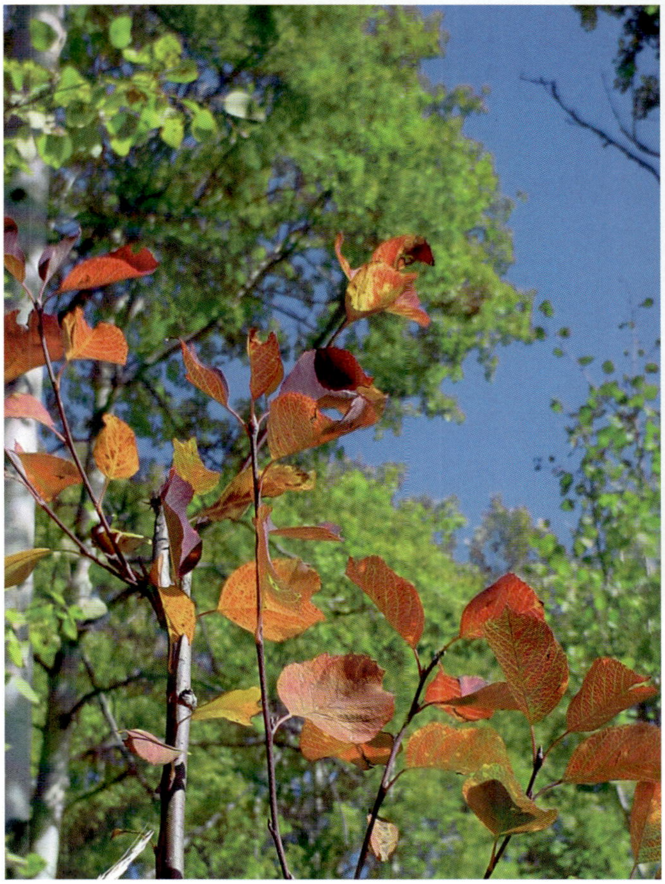

... through the forest ...

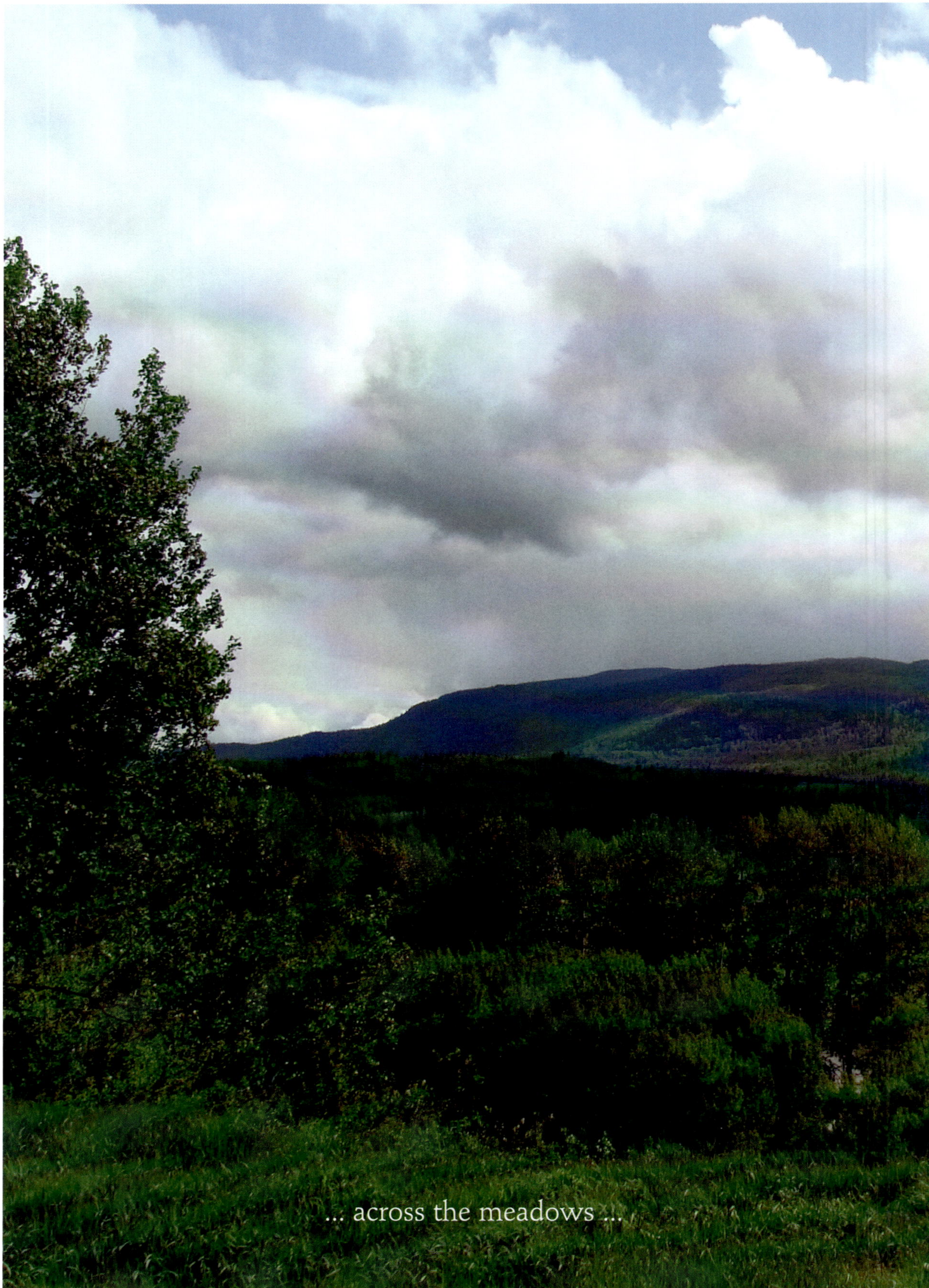
... across the meadows ...

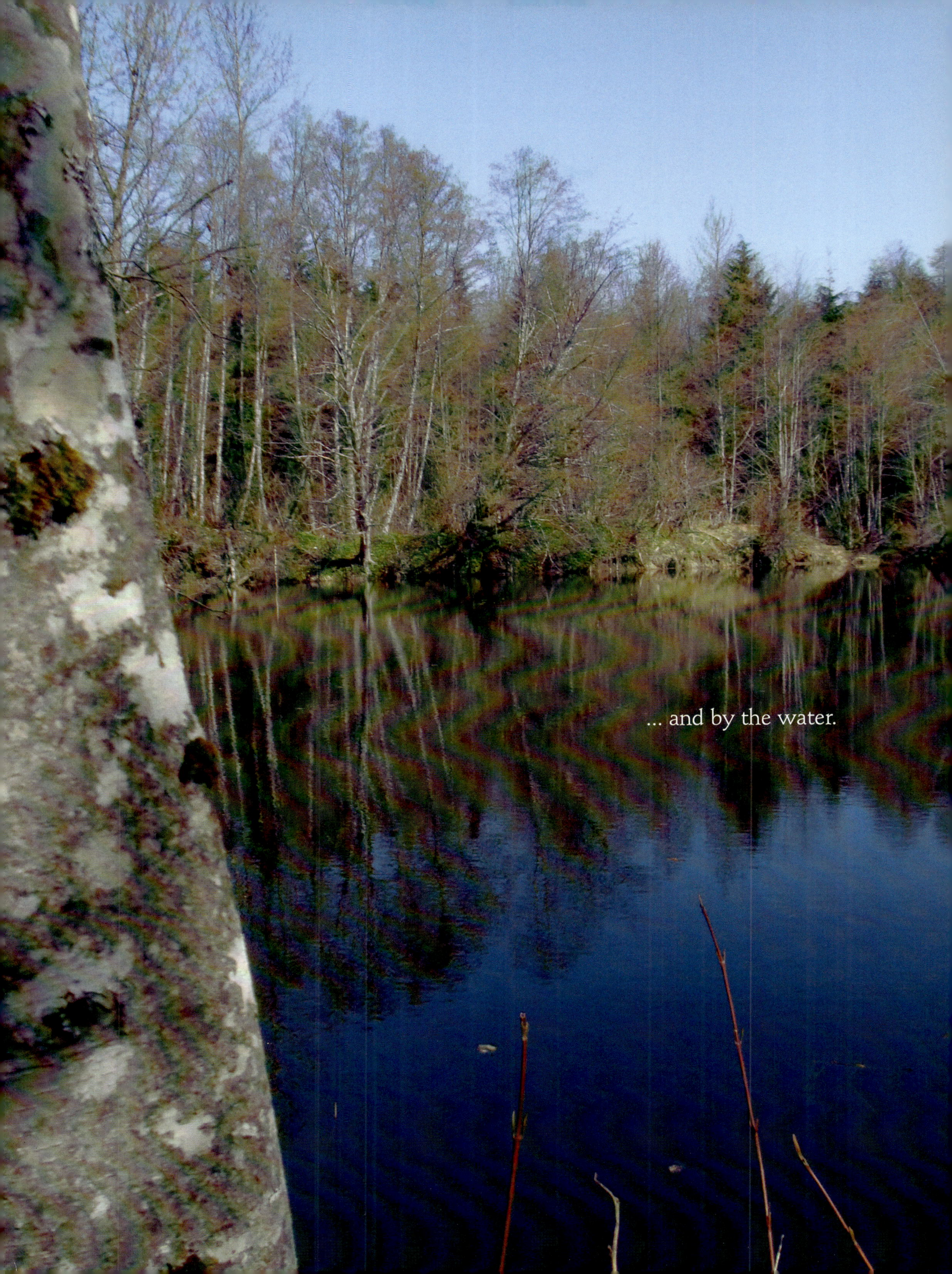
... and by the water.

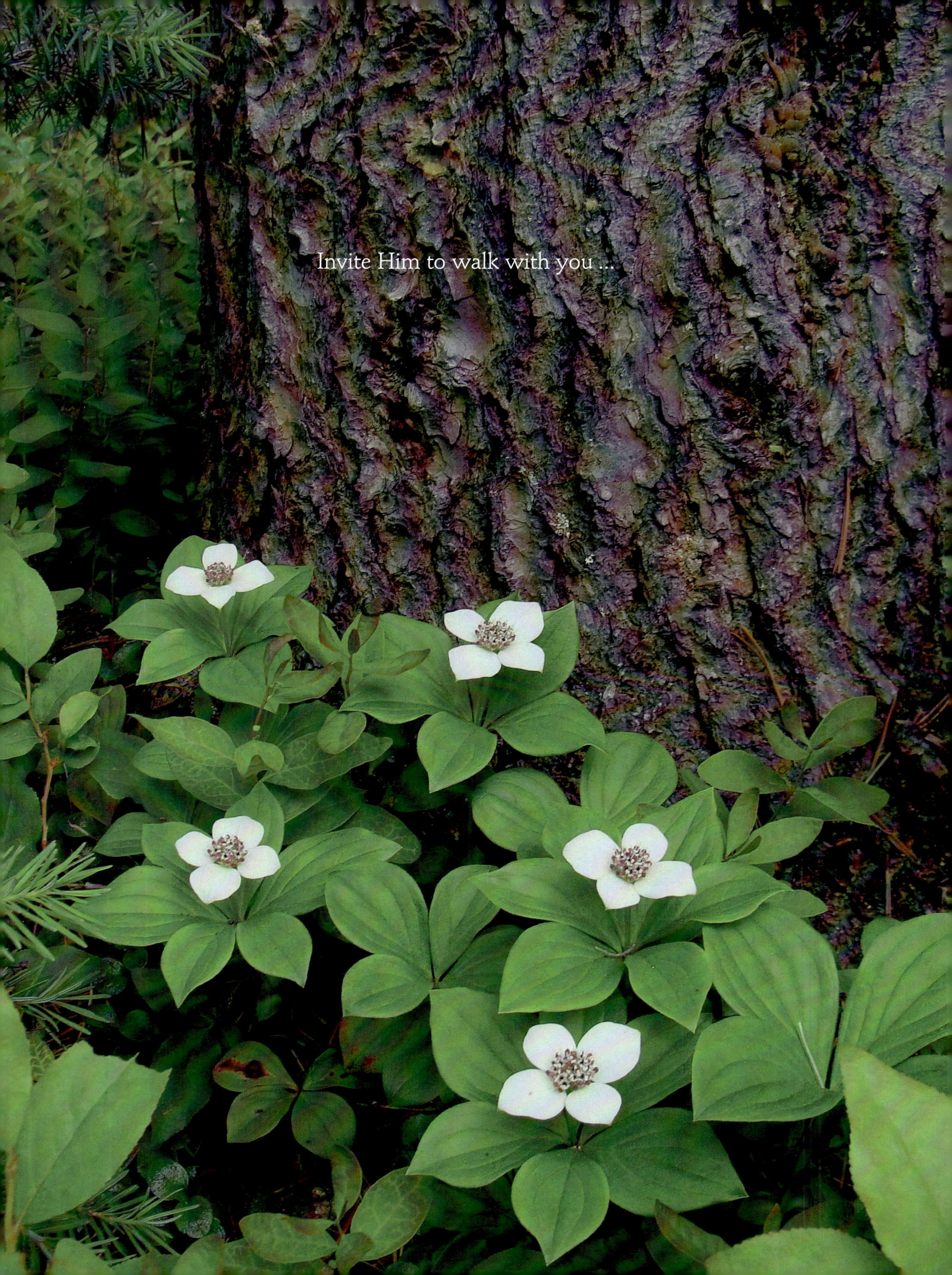

Invite Him to walk with you ...

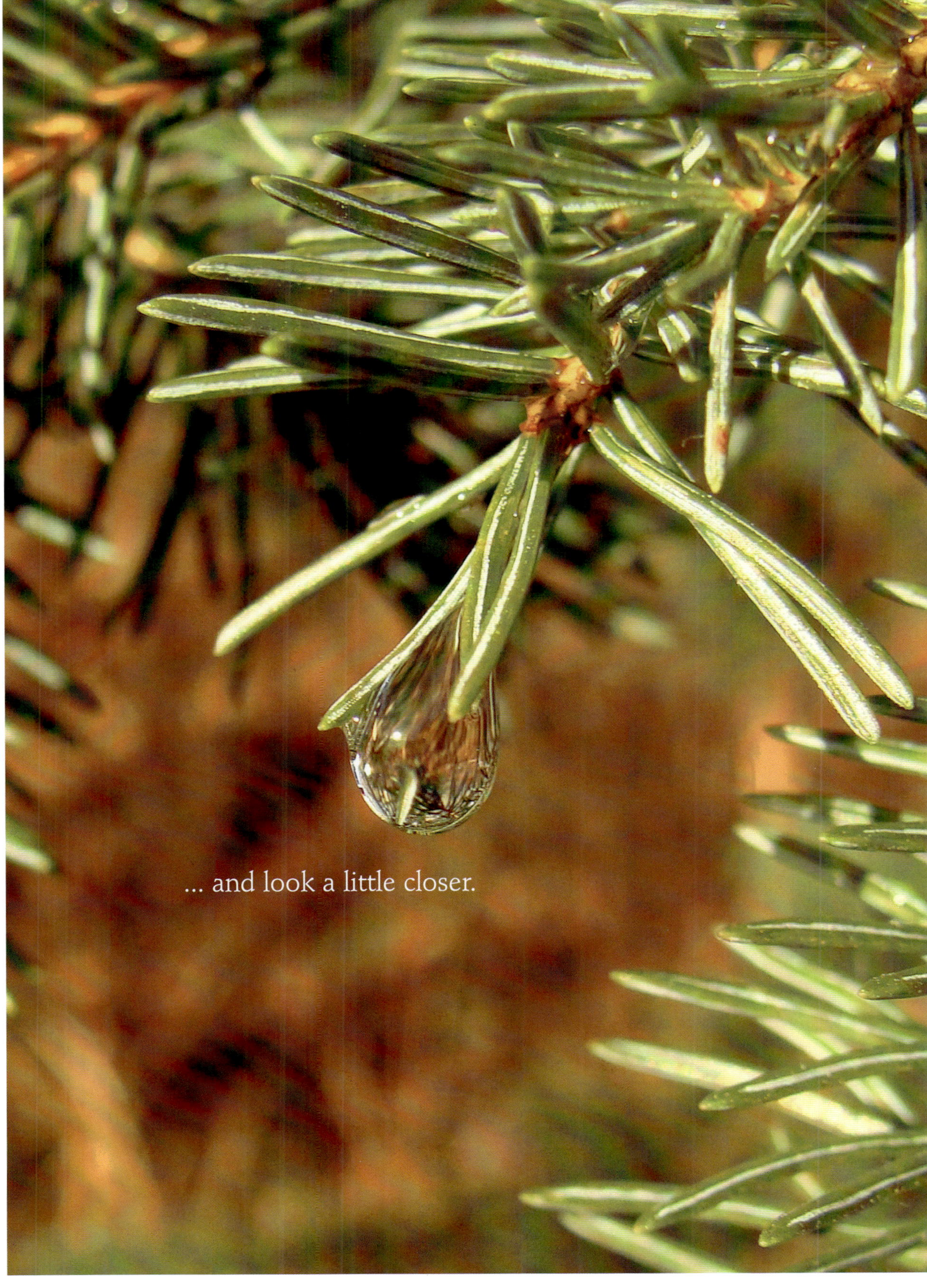
... and look a little closer.